GLOBAL VIEWPOINTS

Citizenship in the 21st Century

Other Books in the Global Viewpoints Series

Anti-Semitism and the Boycott, Divestment, and Sanctions Movement
Chemical and Biological Warfare
Climate Change and Population Displacement
Collective Guilt: Slavery, the Holocaust, and Other Atrocities
The Food Chain: Regulation, Inspection, and Supply
Gender Diversity in Government
Islam in Society
Life After Death? Inheritance, Burial Practices, and Family Heirlooms
Reproductive Rights
The Rise of Authoritarianism
Violence Against Women

GLOBAL VIEWPOINTS

Citizenship in the 21st Century

Martin Gitlin, Book Editor

GREENHAVEN PUBLISHING

Published in 2020 by Greenhaven Publishing, LLC
353 3rd Avenue, Suite 255, New York, NY 10010

First Edition

Articles in Greenhaven Publishing anthologies are often edited for length to meet page requirements. In addition, original titles of these works are changed to clearly present the main thesis and to explicitly indicate the author's opinion. Every effort is made to ensure that Greenhaven Publishing accurately reflects the original intent of the authors. Every effort has been made to trace the owners of the copyrighted material.

Cover image: Spencer Platt/Getty Images
Map: frees/Shutterstock.com

Library of Congress Cataloging-in-Publication Data

Names: Gitlin, Marty, editor.
Title: Citizenship in the 21st century / Martin Gitlin, book editor.
Description: First edition. | New York : Greenhaven Publishing, 2020. | Series: Global viewpoints | Audience: Grades: 9 to 12. | Includes bibliographical references and index.
Identifiers: LCCN 2019002260| ISBN 9781534505513 (library bound) | ISBN 9781534505520 (pbk.)
Subjects: LCSH: World citizenship—Juvenile literature. | World politics—21st century—Juvenile literature. | Globalization—Political aspects.
Classification: LCC JZ1320.4 .C5255 2020 | DDC 323.6/5—dc23
LC record available at https://lccn.loc.gov/2019002260

Manufactured in the United States of America

Website: http://greenhavenpublishing.com

Contents

Chapter 2: Issues That Affect Citizenship in the 21st Century

Chapter 3: The Influence of the Internet on Global Citizenship

Chapter 4: Citizenship of the Future

Foreword

> *"The problems of all of humanity can only be solved by all of humanity."*
> *—Swiss author Friedrich Dürrenmatt*

Global interdependence has become an undeniable reality. Mass media and technology have increased worldwide access to information and created a society of global citizens. Understanding and navigating this global community is a challenge, requiring a high degree of information literacy and a new level of learning sophistication.

Building on the success of its flagship series, Opposing Viewpoints, Greenhaven Publishing has created the Global Viewpoints series to examine a broad range of current, often controversial topics of worldwide importance from a variety of international perspectives. Providing students and other readers with the information they need to explore global connections and think critically about worldwide implications, each Global Viewpoints volume offers a panoramic view of a topic of widespread significance.

Drugs, famine, immigration—a broad, international treatment is essential to do justice to social, environmental, health, and political issues such as these. Junior high, high school, and early college students, as well as general readers, can all use Global Viewpoints anthologies to discern the complexities relating to each issue. Readers will be able to examine unique national perspectives while at the same time appreciating the interconnectedness that global priorities bring to all nations and cultures.

Material in each volume is selected from a diverse range of sources, including journals, magazines, newspapers, nonfiction books, speeches, government documents, pamphlets, organization newsletters, and position papers. Global Viewpoints is truly global, with material drawn primarily from international sources available in English and secondarily from US sources with extensive international coverage.

Features of each volume in the Global Viewpoints series include:

- An **annotated table of contents** that provides a brief summary of each essay in the volume, including the name of the country or area covered in the essay.
- An **introduction** specific to the volume topic.
- A world map to help readers locate the countries or areas covered in the essays.
- For each viewpoint, an **introduction** that contains notes about the author and source of the viewpoint explains why material from the specific country is being presented, summarizes the main points of the viewpoint, and offers three **guided reading questions** to aid in understanding and comprehension.
- **For further discussion** questions that promote critical thinking by asking the reader to compare and contrast aspects of the viewpoints or draw conclusions about perspectives and arguments.
- A worldwide list of **organizations to contact** for readers seeking additional information.
- A **periodical bibliography** for each chapter and a **bibliography of books** on the volume topic to aid in further research.
- A comprehensive **subject index** to offer access to people, places, events, and subjects cited in the text.

Global Viewpoints is designed for a broad spectrum of readers who want to learn more about current events, history, political science, government, international relations, economics, environmental science, world cultures, and sociology—students doing research for class assignments or debates, teachers and faculty seeking to supplement course materials, and others wanting to understand current issues better. By presenting how people in various countries perceive the root causes, current consequences, and proposed solutions to worldwide challenges, Global Viewpoints volumes offer readers opportunities to enhance their global awareness and their knowledge of cultures worldwide.

Introduction

> *"No one is born a good citizen; no nation is born a democracy. Rather, both are processes that continue to evolve over a lifetime. Young people must be included from birth. A society that cuts off from its youth severs its lifeline."*
>
> *—Former United Nations secretary-general Kofi Annan*

The responsibilities of people around the world to maximize positive citizenship comes with much gray area. The depth and courage of action that one can take in seeking to improve his or her society is based on that society itself. Nobody can rightfully compare, for instance, the ability of a citizen to affect change without risk in North Korea and the United States. Those who actively seek freedom of speech and assembly in the former country are likely to wind up in an early grave. Those who carry out their duties as citizens of countries founded on and steeped in freedom can do so without fear. There is indeed no comparison.

The obligation to be an active citizen is universal. But how that citizen contributes to society varies based on issues affecting community and country. The difficulty for people in countries with the harshest governments and regimes to create change is understood. One can argue that as global citizens, it is imperative for those who live in countries that embrace freedom to help those forced to live in darkness further the causes of freedom in their nations.

All problems around the world revolve around the human condition. The rights of those in East Africa to live without war and famine. The rights of Middle Easterners to live without the threat of terrorism. The rights of South Americans to live without governmental instability and gangsterism. The rights of people around the world to clean water without the threat of environmental catastrophe. People everywhere have the power to affect change either individually or through putting pressure on the powers that be. The articles in the four chapters that follow provide wide-ranging ideas and viewpoints regarding the duty of citizens to make a difference at all levels.

The obvious problem with the duty of citizenship is that the actions of those embracing clashing opinions often cause verbal and even physical conflict. One might argue that the necessity and level of positivity of such struggles are based on where they take place. An armed rebellion against an authoritarian regime in a country lacking freedom of speech or assembly might be considered a positive development, whereas in the United States or Europe, civil discourse that can affect change is vastly preferable to the same kind of violent uprising.

Another issue affecting global citizenship is citizenship itself. Throughout many parts of the world, but particularly in western Europe and the United States, refugees seeking a better life have poured over the borders. Many in those countries would prefer the refugees not be offered citizenship. They fear, rightly or wrongly, an increase in crime. They fear the loss of jobs to the newcomers. Americans were told by their own president that the foreigners streaming in from Mexico were murderers and rapists when overwhelming evidence showed that the huge majority were seeking to escape poverty and drug-related violence in their own countries. What is the duty of US citizens, whether they agree or disagree with the assessment of Donald Trump? Should their involvement stop at a Facebook post expressing their opinion? Or should they take stronger action, such as organizing protests?

The answer to all such questions of global citizenship is that the more people get involved, they more they can inspire change. The Internet has shrunk the globe. People have a greater opportunity to express their views and organize. The world can only hope that far more citizens with positive intentions, those who yearn to make their communities and countries healthier and more inclusive places, become more active than those who promote fearmongering and hate.

The authors of the viewpoints in *Global Viewpoints: Citizenship in the 21st Century* provide a wide variety of opinions on the role of citizenship worldwide. The basic idea that one and all should do what they can to create positive developments is unaffected by region. The risks involved and the specific issues needed to be addressed by those citizens vary based on the nations in which they live, the governments that rule them, and the freedoms or lack thereof they are allowed.

One thing is certain. Ideal citizenship does not begin and end in one's community or even in one's country. We are all citizens of the world. It can be argued that the bumper sticker some have on their cars that states "Think Globally" expresses the viewpoint of a model citizen.

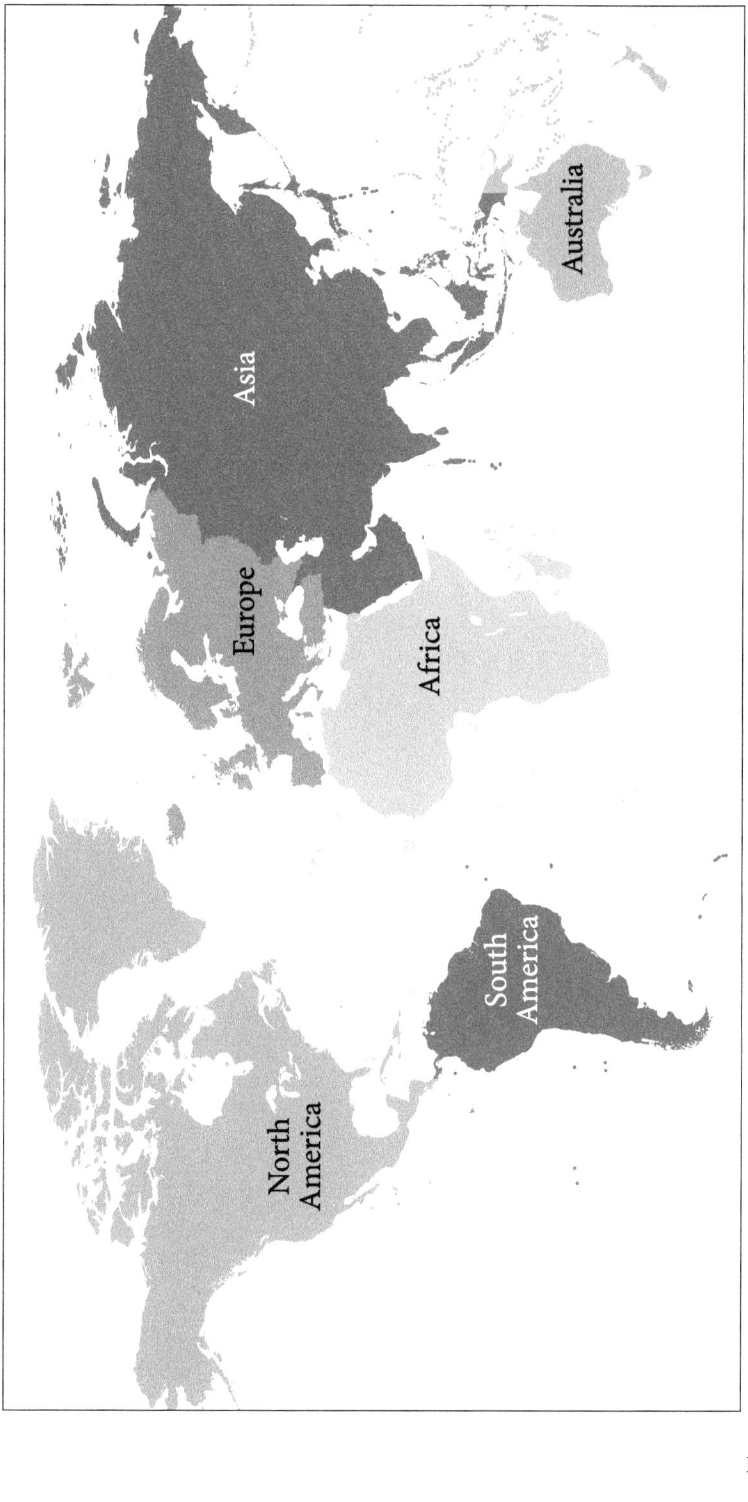
Asia
Europe
Africa
Australia
North America
South America

GLOBAL VIEWPOINTS

Chapter 1

Citizenship Around the World

Viewpoint 1

In the United States, Donald Trump Is Opening Eyes About Birthright Citizenship

Eyder Peralta

In the following viewpoint, Eyder Peralta tackles the topic of birthright citizenship, which was raised in the United States following the rise of businessman and TV personality Donald Trump to the presidency. The author explores the Constitution and American history to provide what he sees as a reminder to readers about what constitutes citizenship. He writes about slavery and the treatment of the American Indian to make points about birthright citizenship and cites issues outside of American soil as well. Peralta is the East Africa correspondent for National Public Radio.

As you read, consider the following questions:

1. What is birthright citizenship?
2. What was the strongest historical reference made here to explain birthright citizenship?
3. Does the author offer an opinion about the state of US politics?

Every few years, the common law concept of *jus soli*—or birthright citizenship—comes back into the news.

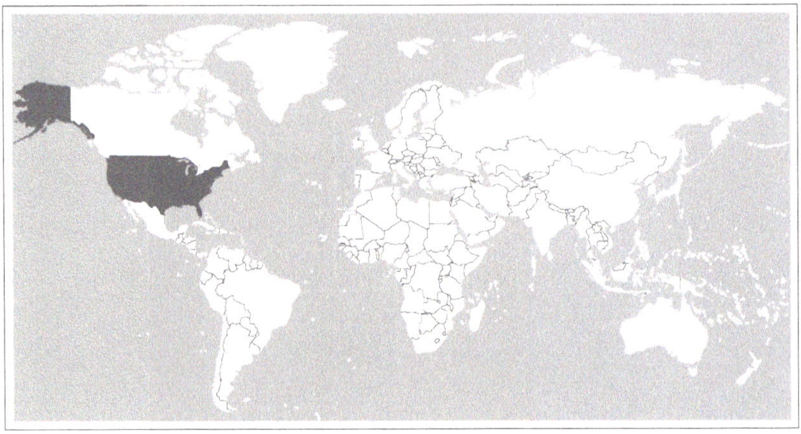

This time, it was thrust onto the stage by Republican presidential candidate Donald Trump, who just unveiled an immigration plan. One of his proposals is to stop automatically giving citizenship to most people born on US soil. Rival GOP candidate Scott Walker issued a similar call.

The concept of *jus soli* has a storied history in the United States that dates to the late 1800s.

Here are three things that will bring you up to speed on the issue:

1. It's in the Constitution

The issue of citizenship was brought into focus by a Supreme Court ruling in 1857 that essentially declared that blacks—even the daughters and sons of freed slaves—were not US citizens.

In 1868, the US ratified the 14th Amendment to the US Constitution. The first sentence reads: "All persons born or naturalized in the United States, and subject to the jurisdiction thereof, are citizens of the United States and of the State wherein they reside."

That language made it clear the Supreme Court's ruling in the *Dred Scott* case was overturned and that black Americans would enjoy US citizenship.

2. It Still Left Some Big, Open Questions

As we've explained in the past, there's one key clause in that sentence from the 14th Amendment—"subject to the jurisdiction thereof"—that left wiggle room for interpretation.

As a Congressional Research Service report from 2010 puts it, what that clause means has been the subject of great debate. Did it mean that the children born to Chinese immigrants—who were once under law not permitted to become naturalized citizens—conferred birthright citizenship? Did it include Native Americans born on sovereign reservations?

All those questions were eventually settled in the 1898 Supreme Court case *United States v. Wong Kim Ark*.

Essentially, the court said the common law concept of *jus soli* should be applied to the 14th Amendment. Congressional Research Service explains:

> "The Court held that the Fourteenth Amendment affirmed the traditional *jus soli* rule, including the exceptions of children born to foreign diplomats, to hostile occupying forces or on foreign public ships, and added a new exception of children of Indians owing direct allegiance to their tribes. It further held that the 'Fourteenth Amendment … has conferred no authority upon Congress to restrict the effect of birth, declared by the Constitution to constitute a sufficient and complete right to citizenship' and that it is 'throughout affirmative and declaratory, intended to allay doubts and settle controversies which had arisen, and not to impose any new restrictions upon citizenship."

In other words, the 14th Amendment excludes children born to diplomats or hostile occupying forces and those born on foreign public ships.

Those are some very narrow restrictions that most legal scholars agree do not exclude the children of illegal immigrants from receiving automatic citizenship. To be clear, it means that current jurisprudence indicates the US-born children of undocumented immigrants are given citizenship by the 14th Amendment.

As for Native Americans, the court ruled that the amendment did not confer birthright citizenship to those born on reservations, because they are not technically subject to US jurisdiction. As Congressional Research Service reports, the Nationality Act of 1940 "finally and unambiguously declared all Native Americans born in the United States to be US citizens."

3. Birthright Citizenship Is a New World Philosophy

As University of California, San Diego sociologist John Skrentny told NPR in 2010, the US is an anomaly in the world when it comes to this issue.

Most of the rest of the world, for example, gives people citizenship based on a concept known as *jus sanguinis*, literally "by right of blood."

"The idea there is that the nation, the people are bonded together through ancestry," Skrentny said. "The other notion of nationhood is generally understood as a civic notion of nationhood. And this is the idea that folks are bonded together by where they are, by locality and by the ideas that they might share. And that's what we have in the United States. There are folks who say that, you know, to be an American is to embrace an idea."

It is, Skrentny added, a philosophy that works well for countries made up of immigrants, such as the US and Canada.

In 2012, the Law Library of Congress took a comprehensive look at France, Germany, Greece, Italy, Portugal, Spain and the UK and found that none of those countries automatically give citizenship to children born to undocumented immigrant parents.

The Center for Immigration Studies, which tends to favor more restrictive immigration policies in the US, took a worldwide look at the issue in 2010 and found that "only 30 of the world's 194 countries grant automatic citizenship to children born to illegal aliens."

Viewpoint 2

In Malta, Passports for a Price Brings into Question the Value of Citizenship

Elizabeth Collett

In the following viewpoint, Elizabeth Collett debates whether the value of citizenship can or should be monetized. She offers several examples in exploring the issue as she spotlights prospective citizens in Malta, eastern Europe, and nations of the European Union. The influx of refugees and others seeking citizenship has been more pronounced in that continent than in any other, though in years after this was written it became a huge controversy in the United States as well. Collett is founding director of the Migration Policy Institute Europe and senior advisor to its Transatlantic Council on Migration, which works to improve integration and immigration policies.

As you read, consider the following questions:

1. Why does the author integrate the country of Malta into the text of this article?
2. How does Collett relate the immigration issue facing European nations to the responsibilities of citizenship?
3. What arguments does the author make for and against the rights of citizenship for migrants?

Originally published by the Migration Policy Institute as Elizabeth Collett, "Valuing Citizenship: A Commodity or an Identity?" Migration information source, January 2014, https://www.migrationpolicy.org/news/valuing-citizenship-commodity-or-identity

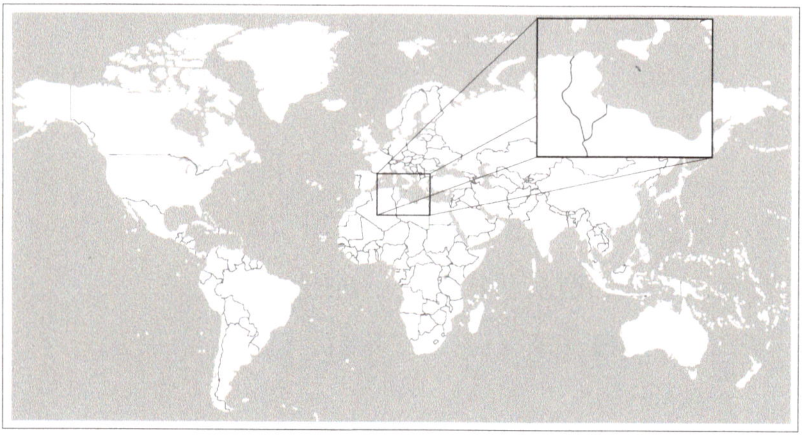

Citizenship, particularly how to acquire it, is a deeply sensitive issue for the European Union, and Member States hold dear their sovereign right to determine who should become a national. Whether, and how, a non-national is allowed to join the national club has also been much debated within national polities. However, there has been strong resistance by Member States towards any discussion of citizenship acquisition at the EU level, despite some outré national policy changes in recent years. A recent decision by Malta's government to sell 1,800 passports (initially for 650,000 euros and later upped to 1.15 million euros in cash and investments) has caused unusual levels of furor in the tiny Mediterranean country, a resolution in the European Parliament, and a move by European Commissioner Viviane Reding to seek legal advice as to whether she has the power to prevent the programme. It would seem that this scheme has become the straw that breaks the camel's back. And if so, why, and is it the price, or the value, of citizenship that is in question?

Citizenship policies vary widely across the European Union. While some Member States set high barriers to acquisition, others have more relaxed approaches. Across Europe, waiting times vary from three to ten years, and some, but by no means all, countries test would-be citizens on their language and civic knowledge.

These policies can be paradoxical and are deeply political. In Italy, a resident immigrant must wait a decade before being able to apply for citizenship. However, descendants of Italian emigrants, with few or no ties, can apply for citizenship without ever needing to set foot in the country. This dichotomy reflects a strong mistrust of immigration to Italy, at odds with the country's proud history of emigration.

At the EU level, citizenship is mostly relevant only as far as it offers a right of free movement and residence across Europe, and EU law is clear that Member States are free to make their own rules as to who is eligible. The rights of free movement have been bitterly debated over the past months, particularly with respect to access to benefits, but the concept of citizenship itself has been left to one side. In 2011, a new Hungarian citizenship law stated that any ethnic Hungarians (descendants of Hungarians who were citizens before 1920), may apply for citizenship, in effect offering citizenship to large numbers of neighbouring state populations, including Moldova, Ukraine, Serbia, Slovakia, and Romania. The new rules reflected the nationalist approach of the ruling government; while they caused a political furor in neighbouring Slovakia, little was said in Brussels.

Responding to criticism, the Maltese government has been at pains to demonstrate its scheme is not unique (and even handed out lists of similar programmes to journalists at a 15 January Parliamentary hearing where the issue was discussed). Indeed, a plethora of investor visa programmes exist in Europe, which offer permanent residence to those willing to deposit large sums of money into property or government bonds, or even a simple bank account. In Latvia, for example, permanent residence could be obtained in 2013 through the purchase of (rural) property to the value of just 72,000 euros, a far lower price than that of the Maltese (the Latvian threshold has now doubled, in part due to public concerns). Whilst only visas and permanent residence are on offer in Latvia, it is implicitly understood that this is also a fast track to citizenship, security, and free movement.

Five Steps Towards Becoming a Global Citizen

1. Understand Global Citizenship

Being a global citizen means living according to values that are good not just for ourselves, or for our own culture, religion or country, but good for the world.

Becoming a global citizen means seeking to understand the world by becoming more aware of global issues. What we do increasingly affects what happens to people in other parts of the world and vice versa. Australia shares responsibility for the global common good. Consumerism and over-consumption rob the poor of their basic necessities. The challenge is to build a sustainable global community founded on interdependence and the principles of human rights.

2. Accept the Challenge to Be a Neighbour

The person, group, or nation in need is our neighbour. We must be ready to voluntarily assist offshore neighbours at times of crisis, and act in the interests of our neighbours who do not share our prosperity and security.

3. Let the World Be a Home in Which All Are Welcome

Strict immigration laws, restrictions on temporary working visas and a harsh policy on asylum seekers are not conducive to offering hospitality and hope to refugees fleeing to our shores in fear of persecution. Generous

But why has the direct valuation of citizenship and its benefits become so repulsive to other policymakers? The number of places on offer is negligible and will not affect free movement flows to any great degree. Presumably, individuals capable of buying their citizenship will not be accessing welfare systems in Malta or elsewhere, and security and criminal checks have been put in place to keep out undesirables. And arguably, the ease with which distant descendants of European emigrés can access citizenship is equally distasteful: allowing those with no links, no term of residence, and no language knowledge to acquire citizenship just as easily, and more cheaply.

development aid and trade practices would assist the United Nations in its efforts to provide for the poor and weak nations of the world.

4. Foster Gospel Nonviolence

Violence threatens not just our human community but our earth as well. Much of the violence in our world is rooted in government policies that ignore the basic needs of the poor and oppressed. By identifying the systems that support war and violence in our world, and educating ourselves about personal, communal and societal nonviolence, we can cultivate a culture of peace. This can begin with something as simple as monitoring the television programs we allow our children to watch. Nationally, we can accept the traditional Catholic doctrine opposing pre-emptive military strikes.

5. Be Globally Environmentally Responsible

The Earth is precious and unique. Environmental responsibility calls us to live by the Earth Charter and to recognise the Kyoto protocol. Indigenous Australians recognise and identify with the spiritual value of the land, which is more than just looking after the land for the sake of what it can give us or enable us to produce. Australia could develop and use the cleanest and safest energy in the world. Individuals could daily reduce their environmental impact.

"Ten Steps Towards Australia Becoming a Global Citizen,"
The Australian Catholic Social Justice Council.

Is the issue one of wealth, and the blunt method in which the Maltese government has distinguished migrants according to their finances? Some have criticised Malta for detaining migrants arriving by boat from North Africa, whilst welcoming those with attractive bank statements. But this too is nothing new. Most countries across the EU apply "selective" immigration policies, preferring those with university degrees and skills, and allowing family migration only when it is clear that the sponsoring individual can support family members financially. Immigration systems across the industrialised world categorise migrants according to desirability and, in the case of asylum seekers and refugees, need. Those with human and financial resources tend to be the most desirable.

In fact, the issue may be deeper, and the Maltese initiative has thrown into relief the nature and value of citizenship in a mobile world. The idea that citizenship is a prize, to be valued and respected, is reflected in the tests immigrants are willing to undergo to qualify, and the ceremonies that many enjoy when citizenship is bestowed. Some rules are needed to ensure that citizenship remains meaningful to those who hold it, even those who have dual- and triple-citizenship. Whilst some may acquire citizenship for the passport (and ensuing visa-free travel), others may be seeking access to secure residence in stable prosperous economies with greater rule of law and less capricious governance. But citizenship is more than immigration policy, and should not be viewed in terms of access alone. Citizenship also creates a contract with the national policy and society, and bestows responsibilities such as political participation, and social contribution. This bond cannot be financially assessed.

The mere fact of placing a price on citizenship can paradoxically devalue it. Investor visas—though requiring money—are intended to draw new residents in, with the hope that they will contribute to the future growth of the country. In the United States, Canada, Australia, and the United Kingdom, consideration has been given to the type of investment, and the multiplier effects of that investment on the local community and national well-being. But citizenship sales require nothing of the recipient beyond cash, whilst offering the most precious thing a country has to give, its identity. An uneven bargain.

Different Nations, Different Viewpoints

Leslie Berestein Rojas

In the following viewpoint, Leslie Berestein Rojas connects an issue that was gaining momentum in the United States at the time this viewpoint was written to events taking place in Europe. The author's focus is citizenship at birth, meaning the legal citizenship of those children born in the United States to illegal aliens. The author does not embrace one side of the debate or the other, but rather explains how other countries around the world define and handle the issue of birthright citizenship. The issue of birthright citizenship would become even more contentious after Donald Trump was elected to the presidency. Rojas serves as the immigration and emerging communities reporter for radio station KPCC in Southern California.

As you read, consider the following questions:

1. How does the author relate the policies of birthright citizenship in other countries to the controversy surrounding the issue in the United States?
2. Does the author hint at a personal perspective, or is the viewpoint a straightforward news story?
3. Why has birthright citizenship become such a major issue in Europe?

"How Citizenship Is Defined Around the World," by Leslie Berestein Rojas, Southern California Public Radio, January 31, 2011. Reprinted by permission.

As immigration-restriction advocates campaign to deny US citizenship to the children of undocumented immigrants, it's worth taking a look at how other nations handle citizenship at birth.

The United States is one of a long list of countries that recognize jus soli (Latin for "right of the soil") citizenship, most commonly known as birthright citizenship. And there is an even longer list of nations that don't.

The vast majority of nations in the Americas recognize jus soli, including Canada, Mexico (which recognizes nationality at birth) and most of Central and South America. Outside of the Americas, however, straightforward jus soli policies are rare. The norm in Europe, Asia and in much of Africa and elsewhere is some form of jus sanguinis (Latin for "right of blood") citizenship, typically granted to children born to a national of that country.

The policies vary widely, and many nations have modified their laws in recent decades. A few examples:

- In Australia, which at one time offered citizenship automatically at birth, moved in 1986 to a system where citizenship is automatic only for children born to at least one Australian citizen or legal permanent resident. However, Australian-born children who are not born citizens automatically become citizens at age 10 if they have lived there most of their lives.
- In France, where jus soli citizenship was once the norm, changes made to the law since 1993 now mean that the French-born children of foreign nationals must request citizenship at a later date in their teens, or upon reaching adulthood.
- In Germany, a strict jus sanguinis policy granted automatic citizenship only to children born to German nationals until 2000, when the law was modified. Today, children born to non-German parents are granted German citizenship at birth if at least one parent has been a legal permanent resident for at least three years, or has lived in Germany for eight years.

These children must later apply to retain German citizenship by age 23.

- In the United Kingdom, changes in the law in 1981 ended a system of straightforward jus soli citizenship. Children born in the UK now only become British citizens automatically if one parent is either a British citizen or legally settled there. The same goes for children born in "qualified territories" of the UK.

How do tighter policies for granting citizenship work out for other countries? As global migration has increased and developed nations continue to import labor, just like the United States, nations that don't offer birthright citizenship have still suffered their own immigration-related woes.

In an essay published last fall in the *Los Angeles Times*, Cal State Long Beach international studies professor Julie M. Weise wrote:

> The children born in Germany of two undocumented parents still are not German citizens at birth. The result is an underground market in fraudulent paternity, in which German men who are citizens—derogatorily known as *imbissvaeter*, or fast-food fathers—claim to be a child's father in exchange for a fee, thus enabling the child to be a German citizen.
>
> Far from promoting the rule of law, Germany's approach to citizenship has created a mess.

Weise pointed to related problems in countries like Japan and Israel, which last summer announced plans to deport hundreds of non-citizen children born in Israel to foreign migrant workers.

And when riots broke out in Paris in 2005 after the accidental electrocution of two teens of African descent, with most the rioters young, second-generation children of immigrants from France's former North African colonies, some critics pointed to a two-tiered system that granted birthright citizenship to other French-born youths, but not these, as part of the underlying social disenfranchisement.

Another issue has been statelessness. Many children born to foreign parents abroad are at least considered nationals of their parents' country by virtue of jus sanguinis (a policy the United States employs), but it doesn't always work this way. From a 2006 Migration Policy Institute report:

> Worldwide, the number of stateless persons is rising. The United Nations defines a stateless person as someone who is not considered a national by any state. The rigid practice of *jus sanguinis* policies can result in statelessness. In other cases, a child with a non-national father born in their mother's country of nationality may be denied that nationality as a result of gender restrictions on the transmission of nationality.
>
> Statelessness also occurs when long-residing ethnic populations have been denied citizenship or have been stripped of citizenship as a result of their racial or ethnic origins.

This has also caused problems for US immigration officials, who have run into trouble deporting stateless people born in countries that did not grant them citizenship at birth, sometimes because the countries their parents came from no longer exist or don't recognize their citizenship. For some (including a German-born man detained San Diego that I once came across), this can mean long periods held in immigrant detention while officials try to figure out what to do with them.

According to the pro-restriction advocacy group Center for Immigration Studies, there are other jus soli nations that are considering tightening their citizenship policies. From a paper published last summer, which also mapped and listed countries by which do and don't recognize birthright citizenship:

> For example, Barbados is struggling with large amounts of immigration (relative to its size), both legal and illegal, and is contemplating ending birthright citizenship for children of illegal aliens. The country initiated an illegal alien amnesty last summer which gave illegal aliens six months to legalize their status. Anyone still in the country illegally after December 1, 2009, faces deportation. The amnesty had a number of conditions,

> and any illegal alien with three or more dependents could not automatically qualify.
>
> Consequently, the question of what to do with children born to illegal aliens became central to political debate. A series of changes have been recommended by the nation's immigration department, and one proposed change is the end of birthright citizenship.

Antigua and Barbuda were also named by CIS as countries contemplating restrictive changes. Countries that were listed as having ended "universal birthright citizenship" since the 1980s included UK, India, Malta, Ireland, New Zealand and most recently the Dominican Republic, with illegal immigration as "the main motivating factor in most countries."

Viewpoint 4

In Indonesia, Understanding Citizen Rights Addresses a Power Imbalance

Leiden University

In the following viewpoint, authors from Leiden University in the Netherlands argue that in Asian nations, particularly Indonesia, it is critical to educate people about governmental affairs that greatly affect them as citizens of those countries. This information is important because, though all citizens in the countries in question have the same rights regarding benefits such as health care and land ownership, they may be unaware of those rights due to a disconnect with their governments and other factors.

As you read, consider the following questions:

1. What country is the focus of this article?
2. Why does the author believe poor people have far less power in dealing with their governments than do those with greater wealth?
3. What issues facing the country in question are most prominently explored in this viewpoint?

Various countries in Asia are in the process of becoming a constitutional state democracy. This process is complex, because whereas on paper all citizens of a nation enjoy the same

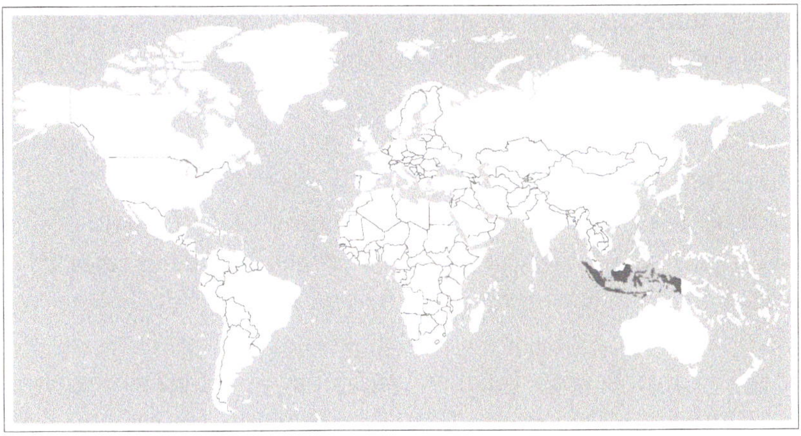

rights, the practice is altogether different. The poor in particular find it difficult to obtain what they are entitled to. This is true in various fields, such as health care, land ownership or divorce. The process is complicated because various different factors are at play, such as ethnic and religious diversity, poor law enforcement, a large distance between central government and the people, and big differences between regions within a country. NGOs and other donors pursue various initiatives to improve the constitutional state democracy and make people's access to the law fairer and more transparent. In order to achieve this, you first need to be aware of the problems that are at play. Strengthening the constitutional state is a complex process. Not only does it entail increasing people's knowledge and skills, it also entails addressing the power imbalance and the various interest structures.

Divorce in Indonesia

PhD candidate Stijn van Huis and Professor of Law and Society in Indonesia Adriaan Bedner investigated the legal status of Indonesian women who divorce and the extent to which these women invoke their rights. "Officially speaking, a divorce can only take place in court. The judge must ensure that women receive maintenance after a divorce, for instance. Many international donors consider access to the courts to be very important, because they assume that poor women in particular are most dependent on the maintenance that their ex pays. We began by questioning the assumptions on which this model is based."

They soon discovered that many women return to their parents after they divorce, because they are better off financially there. Bedner: "Many marriages are for economic reasons. Divorce occurs a lot—particularly in West Java where we conducted our research—and the reason is usually because the husband does not earn enough. In such a case, it does not make much sense for the woman to go to court, because the man cannot pay maintenance anyway."

The next question was what it meant for women who had not divorced in court if they wanted to remarry at a later date. "If there are no children from the second marriage, people often do not consider it necessary to register it. As long as the marriage was concluded according to Islamic rules, the community sees it as valid. But if children are produced in the second marriage, the partners want it to be officially registered to prove that the child was not born out of wedlock. A birth certificate is becoming increasingly important for school places, opening a bank account, marrying, voting, finding a job and welfare and health care. Officially speaking, the Religious Affairs Office is not allowed to register a second marriage if the divorce was not filed in court. What often happens then is that the civil servant registers the new marriage anyway. But if other authorities discover that the registration was not according to the rules, for instance the civil registry office that issues birth certificates, you then have a problem. In that case, many women go to court after all. The court normally grants a retroactive divorce, at least if the official terms have been met. In practice, many problems are thus solved pragmatically."

Encourage or Force People to Go to Court

Many women's rights activists in Indonesia believe that there should be stricter controls on divorce. Some have suggested that retroactive divorce should be banned altogether and that there should be fines for marriages that were not registered according to the rules. The

How Do Americans Stand Out from the Rest of the World?

The differences between America and other nations have long been a subject of fascination and study for social scientists, dating back to Alexis de Tocqueville, the early 19th century French political thinker who described the United States as "exceptional."

Nearly 200 years later, Americans' emphasis on individualism and work ethic stands out in surveys of people around the world. When Pew Research Center surveyed people in 44 countries last spring, 57% of Americans disagreed with the statement "Success in life is pretty much determined by forces outside our control," a higher percentage than most other nations and far above the global median of 38%.

True to the stereotype, surveys showed that Americans are more likely to believe that hard work pays off. When asked, on a scale of 0 to 10, about how important working hard is to getting ahead in life, 73% of Americans said it was a "10" or "very important," compared with a global median of 50% among the 44 nations.

Americans also stand out for their religiosity and optimism, especially when compared with other relatively wealthy countries.

In general, people in richer nations are less likely than those in poorer nations to say religion plays a very important role in their lives. But Americans are more likely than their counterparts in economically advanced nations to deem religion very important. More than half (54%) of Americans said religion was very important in their lives, much higher than the share of people in Canada (24%), Australia (21%) and Germany (21%), the next three wealthiest economies we surveyed from 2011 through 2013.

People in richer nations tend to place less emphasis on the need to believe in God in order to be moral and have good values than people in poorer countries do. While the share of Americans holding that view is far lower than in poorer nations like Indonesia and Ghana (each 99%), the US stands out when compared with people in other economically advanced nations. In the US, 53% say belief in God is a prerequisite for being moral and having good values, much higher than the 23% in Australia and 15% in France, according to our study of 39 nations between 2011 and 2013.

"How Do Americans Stand Out from the Rest of the World?" by George Gao, Pew Research Center, March 12, 2015.

women who call for this are usually middle class and an official divorce is in their interest. Their husbands generally do have an income and a bank account that can be frozen if they fail to pay the maintenance that has been fixed by the court. They also do not want their husbands to secretly enter into polygamous marriage. However, the greater majority of Indonesian women come from the lower classes. They do not need to go to court: the journey costs money, courts are often a long way away and they generally do not stand to gain from going to court.

One of the questions that the government is currently struggling with is whether it should make it more attractive to go to court or whether it should force people to go. To ensure that the discussion is not hijacked, you must be fully aware of the situation, people's motives and the advantages and disadvantages of the various systems. By collaborating with Indonesian researchers, NGOs and the Indonesian government, the researchers ensure that the results of this kind of research are shared and discussed. Bedner: "The women's rights activists that we work with often have very different ideas about the situation at first. We try to use our findings to convince them to seek alternatives."

Periodical and Internet Sources Bibliography

The following articles have been selected to supplement the diverse views presented in this chapter.

Michael Alpert, "Responsibility of Global Citizens," Classroom. https://www.theclassroom.com/responsibilities-of-global-citizens-12082310.html.

Scott Carlin, "The Role of Civil Society in Advancing Global Citizenship," *UN Chronicle*, January 2018. https://unchronicle.un.org/article/role-civil-society-advancing-global-citizenship.

Julie Hirschfeld Davis, "President Wants to Use Executive Order to End Birthright Citizenship," *New York Times*, October 30, 2018. https://www.nytimes.com/2018/10/30/us/politics/trump-birthright-citizenship.html.

Ronald C. Israel, "What Does It Mean to Be a Global Citizen?," *Kosmos Journal*, Spring/Summer 2012. https://www.kosmosjournal.org/article/what-does-it-mean-to-be-a-global-citizen.

Dara Lind, "Birthright Citizenship, Explained," Vox, October 30, 2018. https://www.vox.com/2018/7/23/17595754/birthright-citizenship-trump-14th-amendment-executive-order.

Sudha Sreenivasa Reddy, "Global Citizenship Education: Towards Globalizing Culture of Rights and Responsibilities," *Global Education Magazine*, December 5, 2015. http://www.globaleducationmagazine.com/global-citizenship-education-globalizing-culture-rights-responsibilities.

Ragika Shanmuganathan, "My Roles and Responsibilities as a Global Citizen," Prezi, April 22, 2016. https://prezi.com/5xpd66bhhqsr/my-roles-and-responsibilities-as-a-global-citizen.

Paul Sherman, "Why the World Needs More Global Citizens," Conversation, September 28, 2017. https://theconversation.com/why-the-world-needs-more-global-citizens-84680.

GLOBALVIEWPOINTS

Chapter 2

Issues That Affect Citizenship in the 21st Century

Viewpoint 1

In Europe, an Influx of Immigrants Stokes Fear of Terrorism

Richard Wike, Bruce Stokes, and Katie Simmons

In the following viewpoint, Richard Wike, Bruce Stokes, and Katie Simmons analyze and provide context to Pew Research polling of Europeans that showed their level of fear and apprehension over Muslim immigration from poorer Middle Eastern nations. Among the interesting tidbits from that polling is that those from formerly Communist countries in the Soviet sphere expressed a higher level of fear of terrorism than their counterparts from nations steeped in freedom and democracy. They also expressed a stronger belief that immigrants will take their jobs and social benefits. Wike is director of global attitudes research at Pew Research Center. Stokes is director of global economic attitudes at Pew Research Center. Simmons is associate director of research at Pew Research Center.

"Europeans Fear Wave of Refugees Will Mean More Terrorism, Fewer Jobs," by Richard Wike, Bruce Stokes, and Katie Simmons, July 11, 2016.

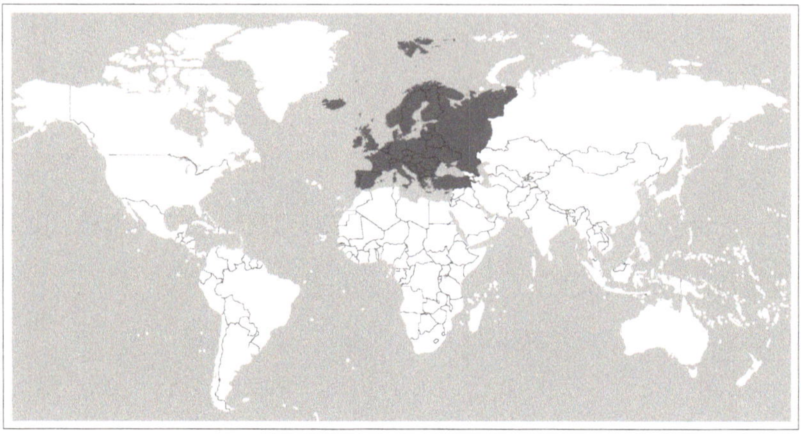

As you read, consider the following questions:

1. Why do you think people in countries formerly in the sphere of the Soviet Union, such as Hungary and Poland, are more fearful of immigrants than those in other European countries?
2. Do the authors make any analysis, or is this just a statistical analysis piece?
3. What are some of the perceptions of Muslims that cloud the opinions of Europeans about immigration, according to this viewpoint?

The recent surge of refugees into Europe has featured prominently in the anti-immigrant rhetoric of right-wing parties across the Continent and in the heated debate over the UK's decision to exit the European Union. At the same time, attacks in Paris and Brussels have fueled public fears about terrorism. As a new Pew Research Center survey illustrates, the refugee crisis and the threat of terrorism are very much related to one another in the minds of many Europeans. In eight of the ten European nations surveyed, half or more believe incoming refugees increase the likelihood of terrorism in their country.

But terrorism is not the only concern people have about refugees. Many are also worried that they will be an economic burden. Half or more in five nations say refugees will take away jobs and social benefits. Hungarians, Poles, Greeks, Italians and French identify this as their greatest concern. Sweden and Germany are the only countries where at least half say refugees make their nation stronger because of their work and talents. Fears linking refugees and crime are much less pervasive, although nearly half in Italy and Sweden say refugees are more to blame for crime than other groups.

Most of the recent refugees to Europe are arriving from majority-Muslim nations, such as Syria and Iraq. Among Europeans, perceptions of refugees are influenced in part by negative attitudes toward Muslims already living in Europe. In Hungary, Italy, Poland and Greece, more than six-in-ten say they have an unfavorable opinion of the Muslims in their country—an opinion shared by at least one-in-four in each nation polled.

For some Europeans, negative attitudes toward Muslims are tied to a belief that Muslims do not wish to participate in the broader society. In every country polled, the dominant view is that Muslims want to be distinct from the rest of society rather than adopt the nation's customs and way of life. Six-in-ten or more hold this view in Greece, Hungary, Spain, Italy and Germany. Notably, the percentage saying that Muslims want to remain distinct has actually declined since 2005 in four out of five countries where trend data are available. The biggest drop has been in Germany, where the share of the public expressing this view has declined from 88% to 61%.

While most Europeans think the recent surge of refugees could lead to more terrorism, there is less alarm that Muslims already living on the Continent might sympathize with extremists. The percentage of the public saying that most or many Muslims in their country support groups like ISIS is less than half in every nation polled. Still, 46% of Italians, 37% of Hungarians, 35% of Poles and 30% of Greeks think Muslims in their countries are favorably inclined toward such extremist groups. On these and other questions included on the poll, Greece, Hungary, Italy and Poland often stand out for expressing greater concern and more negative views about refugees and minority groups.

Across the EU nations surveyed, the refugee crisis has brought into sharp relief deep ideological divides over views of minorities and diversity. On nearly all of the questions analyzed in this report, people on the ideological right express more concerns about refugees, more negative attitudes toward minorities and less enthusiasm for a diverse society.

For example, negative opinions about Muslims are much more common among respondents who place themselves on the right of the ideological spectrum. In Greece, 81% of those on the right express an unfavorable view of Muslims, compared with 50% of those on the left. Significant right-left gaps in attitudes toward Muslims are also found in Germany, Italy, the Netherlands, Sweden, Spain, France and the United Kingdom.

Similarly, supporters of far-right political parties hold much more negative attitudes toward refugees and Muslims and are much more skeptical about the benefits of a diverse society. For instance, fears that the surge of refugees will lead to more terrorism and harm the economy are considerably more widespread among supporters of the UK Independence Party (UKIP) in the UK and the National Front in France.

Ideology is not the only dividing line in European attitudes, however. On many questions, education and age also matter, with older people and less-educated individuals expressing more negative opinions about refugees and minorities.

These are among the key findings from a new survey by Pew Research Center, conducted in ten European Union nations and the United States among 11,494 respondents from April 4 to May 12, 2016, before the Brexit referendum in the UK and terrorist attacks at the Istanbul Atatürk Airport, both of which took place in late June. The survey includes countries that account for 80% of the EU-28 population and 82% of the EU's gross domestic product.

Along with worries about refugees and minorities, the survey finds mixed views regarding the overall value of cultural diversity. When asked whether having an increasing number of people of many different races, ethnic groups and nationalities in their country makes their society a better place to live, a worse place or does not make much difference either way, over half of Greeks and Italians and about four-in-ten Hungarians and Poles say growing diversity makes things worse.

Relatively few Europeans believe diversity has a positive impact on their countries. At 36%, Sweden registers the highest percentage that believes an increasingly diverse society makes their country a better place to live. In many countries, the prevailing view is that diversity makes no difference in the quality of life.

Negative Attitudes Toward Minorities Common in Many Nations

Muslims are not the only minority group viewed unfavorably by substantial percentages of Europeans. In fact, overall, attitudes toward Roma are more negative than attitudes toward Muslims. Across the ten nations polled, a median of 48% express an unfavorable opinion of Roma in their country. Fully 82% hold this view in Italy, while six-in-ten or more say the same in Greece, Hungary and France. Negative views of Roma have gone up since 2015 in Spain (+14 percentage points), the UK (+8) and Germany (+6). Greeks have also become increasingly unfavorable (+14 points) since 2014, the last time Greece was included in the survey.

Negative ratings for Muslims have also increased over the past 12 months in the UK (+9 percentage points), Spain (+8) and Italy (+8), and are up 12 points in Greece since 2014. In France—where coordinated terrorist attacks by ISIS at the Bataclan concert hall and elsewhere in Paris in November left 130 people dead—unfavorable opinions are up slightly since last year (+5 points).

Negative attitudes toward Jews are much less common. A median of only 16% have an unfavorable opinion of Jews in their country. Still, a majority of Greeks give Jews in their country a negative rating, and one-in-five or more express this view in Hungary, Poland, Italy and Spain. Unfavorable attitudes toward Jews have been relatively stable since 2015.

Language, Customs and Tradition Seen as Central to National Identity

Opinions vary about the key components of national identity, but European publics clearly agree that language is fundamental. Across the ten EU countries surveyed, a median of 97% think that being able to speak the national language is important for truly being able to identify with their nationality. A median of 77% say this is very important. Majorities believe it is very important in every nation polled.

There is also a strong cultural component to national identity. A median of 86% believe sharing national customs and traditions is important, with 48% saying this is very important. Fully 68% in Hungary say sharing national customs and traditions is very important for being truly Hungarian, and 66% express similar sentiments in Greece. In contrast, fewer than four-in-ten consider sharing these traditions and customs very important in the Netherlands (37%), Germany (29%) and Sweden (26%).

There is less agreement about the need to be born in a given country. Still, a median of 58% say it is important for someone to be born in a country to be truly considered a national of that country; a third think this is very important. Religion is generally seen as less central to national identity. However, it is an essential factor to many in Greece, where 54% say it is very important to be Christian to be truly Greek.

To further explore this topic, we constructed an index based on the four questions we asked regarding national identity (importance of speaking the national language, sharing customs, being native born and being Christian). The results highlight the extent to which exclusionary views vary across the EU. By far, restrictive views are most common in Hungary, Greece, Poland and Italy; they are least common in Sweden, Germany and the Netherlands.

VIEWPOINT 2

In Europe, Immigration Can Balance an Aging Population

Ben Hall

In the following viewpoint, Ben Hall argues that Europe's low birthrate and aging population could benefit from a spike in immigration. Hall examines migration issues in many European countries, including France, Sweden, Holland, Belgium, Great Britain, Germany, Austria, and Switzerland. Much has changed since this viewpoint was written, as immigration from the Middle East has greatly intensified. But Hall wrote about many of the same problems and challenges Europeans and their countries experienced then as they do nearly two decades later. Hall is Europe editor at the Financial Times *and a former research director of the Centre for European Reform.*

As you read, consider the following questions:

1. How has the immigration issue in Europe changed since this article was written in 2000?
2. How does the author use statistics to explain the rise of multiculturalism in the European Union?
3. What conclusions does Hall draw about the future of European immigration?

Europe's history has been shaped by migration. For centuries, merchants, craftsmen and intellectuals crossed the continent to practice their trades or start new lives. Millions emigrated from

"Immigration in the European Union: Problem or Solution?" by Ben Hall, Prospect Magazine, June 2000. Reprinted by permission.

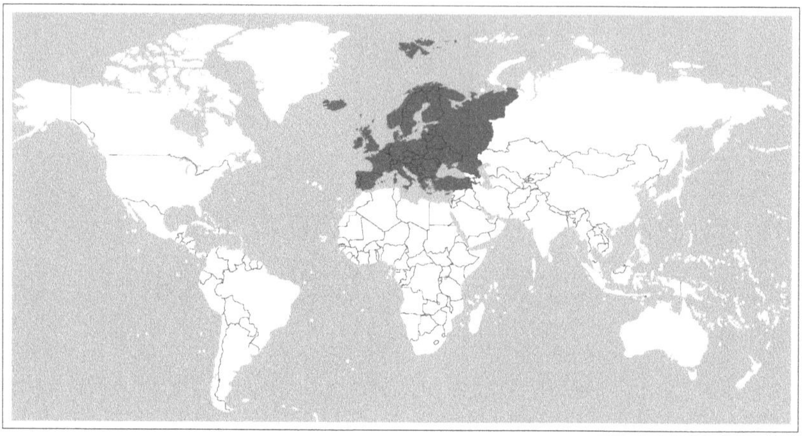

Europe, first to the colonies and later to the Americas and the Antipodes. Europe also has a long history of forced migration: from the expulsion of the Jews from Spain to the population shifts in southeast Europe caused by the many wars between the Russian, Austro-Hungarian and Ottoman empires.

Large-scale immigration into western Europe is more recent. From 1960 to 1973, the number of foreign workers in western Europe doubled from 3 to 6% of the workforce. It was highest in places like the UK and France, with relatively open access for citizens of their former colonies; in Germany, too, the number of foreigners (nearly half Turks) rose 4m in the 25 years after 1960, although they seldom became citizens. But primary immigration into Europe—driven by labour needs—all but ended with the oil crisis of 1973. The foreign-born population has continued to grow, not least because most countries still issue tens of thousands of residence permits each year for the purposes of family reunification (nearly 80% of the 58,700 people accepted for permanent settlement in the UK in 1997 were wives and children). EU countries also issue thousands of work permits each year. In Britain in 1997, nearly half of the 54,000 permits went to Americans and Japanese mainly in highly skilled jobs; elsewhere in Europe the permits often go to seasonal farm workers. But the proportion of foreign-born residents in the EU remains low, ranging from 9% in Austria, Belgium and Germany, to under 2% in Spain.

Since the late 1980s, the number of people applying for asylum has increased sharply. In 1984 there were only 104,000 applications in western Europe. This figure grew to 692,000 in 1992 and then declined during much of the 1990s. Numbers grew again to 350,000 in 1998 and about 400,000 in 1999, although this year they have begun to fall away. Thus asylum has become one of the principal means of immigration into the EU.

Why this sudden surge? The end of the Cold War lifted the lid on a number of small wars and ethnic conflicts around the world. In this type of warfare, the combatants—regular troops complimented by paramilitaries—often target civilian populations. Many people applying for asylum are ostensibly fleeing such "ethnic cleansing," most notably in Bosnia in the early 1990s and Kosovo in the late 1990s. Also, with the end of communist rule many eastern Europeans believe that their aspirations for a better life can only be served in the west. With freer movement and cheaper travel, it is not surprising that many have tried to emigrate westward. The problem is that tens of thousands have tried to use the asylum process to do so, leading to a backlash, in some countries, against all types of migrants.

The top six countries from which British asylum-seekers came last year were China, Somalia, Sri Lanka, Yugoslavia, Poland and Afghanistan. But most of the world's refugees do not get to Europe. They remain in the region close to their countries, often in camps. Iran was housing some 1.9m refugees in 1998, mostly from Iraq and Afghanistan, and there are some 2m Afghan and Iraqi refugees in Pakistan.

But in some EU states, asylum has become a totemic issue. It overlaps with other emotional matters such as ethnicity and identity, revealing an illiberal streak in liberal democracies. But we should keep things in perspective. It may have been easier for migrants to enter the UK 100 years ago, but once there they were

Ignoring Atrocities in the Congo

Some lives matter more than others: the "hierarchy of death," they call it. The millions killed, maimed and traumatised in the Democratic Republic of Congo are surely at the bottom of this macabre pile. The country was the site of the deadliest war since the fall of Adolf Hitler, and yet I doubt most people in the west are even aware. No heart-wrenching exclusives at the top of news bulletins; no calls for western militaries to "do something."

We are rightly appalled at a barbaric conflict in Syria that has stolen the lives of 200,000 civilians; and yet up to 6 million people are believed to have perished in the DRC. Not that the mainstream media alone can be berated for this astonishing lack of attention. Although the murderous intensity of the war peaked between 1998 and 2003, the misery has persisted. According to Oxfam, civilians in the east of the country still face exploitation at the hands of armed groups. The UN has labelled the country "the rape capital of the world." Women, girls and boys have been systematically raped as a weapon of war. Back in 2011, it was estimated that 48 women were raped every hour in the country. Men were raped, too: there are stories of men being raped three times a day for three years. Then there's the cannibalism: at one point, pygmies in the north east were being killed and eaten by rebels.

It was a war that was remorseless when it came to the innocent: when 45,000 people were being killed every month, around half of them were small children, even though they only represented a fifth of the population. The war triggered devastating waves of starvation and disease which claimed the lives of millions.

Armed militias continue to commit atrocities, and the aftermath of the war has left the country impoverished and devastated. And yet this vast country of nearly 80 million people barely punctures our consciousness. Why?

We should perhaps just be more honest. On another continent, such a devastating war would never have been allowed to rage for so long. African lives simply do not matter enough: a death toll of up to 6 million would surely not have been tolerated elsewhere.

"Let's Be Honest. We Ignore Congo's Atrocities Because It's in Africa," by Owen Jones, The Guardian, *March 6, 2015.*

far more likely to face violence and had nothing like the legal and social protection of today's welfare states. None the less, resentment of "the other" can be exploited by demagogues, especially when there is no obvious gap in the job market for refugees to fill. Overall, refugees are only a small burden on taxpayers—but this may not be how it seems in areas of high refugee density (in Britain this means a few London boroughs or towns like Dover), where migrants share services such as schools, hospitals and housing with the poorest locals.

A Pan-European Issue

Most people think about the asylum issue in domestic terms, but it is pan-European. Across the continent, the policy issues and the debate are remarkably similar. Even Ireland, whose modern history is one of mass emigration, saw asylum applications leap from 39 in 1992 to more than 4,600 in 1998. Some countries have experienced much larger increases than others. Germany has consistently received more refugees than other EU countries—more than 60% of all those who applied for asylum in western Europe in 1992. Austria, Holland, Sweden and Switzerland have, at times during the last decade, received high numbers of refugees per head of their populations, while some of the larger states, especially France, Italy and Spain, have received relatively fewer. Britain is in the middle of the field. It had 17,000 applications in 1989 and 71,000 a decade on—more than Germany. The largest annual tally was 73,000 in 1991, under a Conservative government.

There are, of course, nuances in the tone of the debate and the policy framework in different states. But the stress everywhere has been on reducing the flow, while trying to distinguish genuine asylum-seekers from purely "economic" migrants. The Bonn government responded to the Balkan influx in the early 1990s—and to some attacks on refugees—by tightening its previously liberal asylum law. This introduced a "safe third country" rule: if a person has passed through a country which Germany deems safe, he or she cannot apply for asylum in Germany. Since Germany considers all neighbouring countries as safe, asylum-seekers who do not arrive by plane are likely to be rejected.

After these restrictions were introduced in 1993, the number of applications fell sharply, prompting other EU states to follow. In Holland, the numbers of asylum-seekers rose considerably after 1996. The Dutch authorities (like the British, see below) are experiencing difficulties in dealing quickly with applications. As in Britain, Dutch politicians talk of the "flood" of "bogus" refugees, although Dutch newspapers use more temperate language than the British tabloids.

The Dutch government has devised a new Aliens Act, due to come into effect next year. The law, which has been hotly debated, is designed to streamline the asylum procedure and reduce the average time for processing applications from 22 months to six. It will also give all asylum-seekers (who are eligible to stay) a more temporary status. Instead of giving full refugee status after the initial procedure, each case will be reviewed after three years, and only then approved or rejected.

In some countries, asylum is only one element in a wider debate about immigration and national identity. Jörg Haider's far-right Freedom party exploited Austrians' unease about immigrants and refugees to manoeuvre itself into the federal government.

In Italy, the biggest issues are what to do with the large number of illegal immigrants or clandestini already in the country, how to tackle the large-scale trafficking of migrants, particularly by speed-boat from Albania, and concern at the involvement of the mafia in the smuggling gangs. Silvio Berlusconi, leader of the right-wing Forza Italia, and Umberto Bossi, leader of the Lega Nord, successfully fought April's regional elections on a stringent anti-immigration, anti-asylum platform.

But, for a number of reasons, Italy has tended to receive small numbers of asylum applications. Many refugees, particularly from Somalia and the former Yugoslavia, are given work permits on humanitarian grounds, which relieves them of the need to apply for asylum. Periodic amnesties for illegal immigrants means that they can regularise their situation rather than apply for refugee status. And many migrants use Italy as a port of entry, travelling on to Germany, Switzerland or Britain, where they enter clandestinely (often in lorries) or apply for asylum.

In France and Spain, which receive few asylum-seekers relative to the Netherlands, Britain and Germany, asylum has not been such a big issue. In France, the Front National, wracked by infighting, has lost its way. Government attempts to deport illegal immigrants—provoking hunger strikes and demonstrations—have subsided. Integrating existing immigrants and regularising the situation of the sans papiers, many of whom may have been resident in France for years, now dominates the debate on immigration.

It is obviously beyond the immediate power of the EU to eradicate the root causes of all migration. But over time, if the EU wants to reduce migratory pressure, it will have to provide more development aid, debt relief, and fair trade, and it will need to be better equipped to prevent conflict and keep the peace in trouble spots around the world. These objectives lie at the heart of the EU's common foreign and security policy. (The EU's resolute position in the Kosovo crisis no doubt owed much to a fear of a mass exodus of Kosovan refugees.)

Comparing Europe and the US

But should European states even try to stop economic migration? Europe's population is set to decline over the next 50 years. Italy will lose 28% of its population by 2050. In order to maintain its working age population, Italy would need to start importing more than 350,000 immigrants per year or, alternatively, keep its citizens working until they are 75.

The US (population 275m) has tended to take only small numbers of asylum-seekers—fewer than Europe, relative to its population. But it has a more liberal immigration regime. By the late 1990s, the US was taking in about 1m immigrants a year: 730,000 legal immigrants, 200,000 illegal aliens and about 100,000 refugees. About 70% of legal immigrants are admitted for the purposes of family reunification.

The in-flows of migrants during the 1980s and 1990s—the second great migration of the 20th century—has literally changed the face of America. In 1970 the US population was 5% Hispanic, 1% Asian and 12% black. A recent projection indicates that by 2050, it will be 26% Hispanic, 8% Asian and 14% black.

Immigration in the US is embraced more enthusiastically by the free market right than the trade union left, but it has brought real benefits. Immigrants contribute to innovation—witness the number of foreigners in Silicon Valley. And they do jobs that native workers refuse, such as sustaining Californian agriculture. But in his new book, *Heaven's Door*, Harvard economist George Borjas claims that the economic benefits brought by the latest 20-year wave of immigrants are more disputable. He points to the fall-off in skills relative to those who emigrated to the US in the 1950s and 1960s. He argues that America should admit only 500,000 immigrants per year, and select the most highly skilled. These are criteria which, he acknowledges, would have prevented him, a refugee from Cuba, from immigrating in the early 1960s.

Congress recently approved an extra 200,000 visas for skilled workers. European governments are taking similar steps. Germany wants 20,000 information technology workers from outside Europe, particularly software engineers from India (prompting the Christian Democrats to campaign on the slogan Kinder statt Inder, "children not Indians"). Britain, too, wants to recruit east European computer experts but is only too keen to turn away their less skilled compatriots.

No one knows what will happen to asylum trends—indeed, no one knows what is really happening now; one reputable estimate puts the number of illegal migrants smuggled into the EU each year as 400,000. The probability is that more small wars and the increasing urbanisation of the world's population will keep the asylum numbers high. But immediate attention in Europe is likely to shift back to more conventional labour-shortage recruitment. There will be no return to the open door policy of the 1960s (let alone the 19th century), but the EU economy will require an increase in selective primary immigration.

Viewpoint 3

In East Africa, Millions Are Experiencing the Threat of Famine

Chris Huber and Kathryn Reid

In the following viewpoint, Chris Huber and Kathryn Reid write about war-related famine in East Africa that has taken millions of lives and make pleas for greater awareness and aid from citizens around the world. Among the other issues contributing to the catastrophe in East Africa are drought and exorbitant food prices that fall beyond the budget of many in the region. The authors cite what they see as the most tragic aspect of the disasters, which is the loss of life of children too young to understand the issues involved. Huber and Reid are on the staff of World Vision, a global Christian humanitarian organization that seeks an end to global poverty and injustice.

As you read, consider the following questions:

1. Do you believe famine and starvation are the worst of all human tragedies on earth?
2. According to the authors, when and what were the roots of this crisis in Africa?
3. Do the authors provide a plan to solve or at least help alleviate this problem?

"East Africa Hunger, Famine: Facts, FAQs, and How to Help," by World Vision, with contributions from Chris Huber and Kathryn Reid, July 10, 2018. Reprinted by permission. The crisis in east Africa is ongoing. Please visit https://www.worldvision.org/hunger-news-stories/east-africa-hunger-famine-facts.

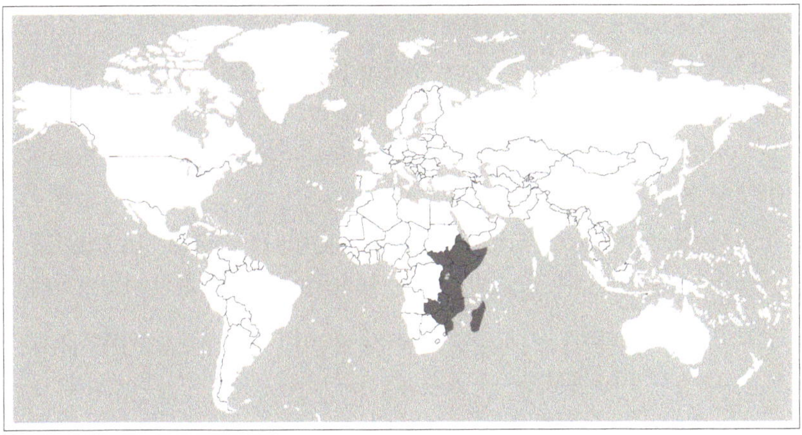

Millions of people in East Africa are experiencing chronic hunger and the threat of famine. Conflict, recurring severe drought, and high food prices are to blame. In a recent development, more than 800,000 people have fled their homes due to violence in south Ethiopia since the beginning of 2018. They are in desperate need of assistance.

South Sudan, Somalia, and Ethiopia are facing high levels of food insecurity in various parts of their countries over the next few months. About 22 million people in East Africa need help to secure their livelihoods and acquire adequate food. Nine million children are in need of nutrition assistance.

Recurring East Africa droughts make it difficult for farmers and herders to produce crops and feed livestock. Seasonal rainfall has been above average in some places, and excessive amounts of rain falling on drought-stricken land have resulted in flash floods, killing more than 300 people and washing away crops and shelters.

Children are the worst affected, with their health and development drastically impacted. More than 15 million children in Ethiopia, Kenya, South Sudan, and Somalia are struggling to get enough to eat. Floods are increasing the risk of cholera and other water-related diseases among people with temporary shelter and poor sanitation.

Brief History of Hunger and Famine in Africa

A look back at some of Africa's major food crises shows conditions still faced by many Africans today: poverty, drought, conflict, and environmental degradation due to overgrazing, deforestation, and other types of environmental damages.

- 1968 to 1980s—A drought in the Sahel region led to 1 million deaths in Mali, Chad, Niger, Mauritania, and Burkina Faso.
- 1980 to 1981—Drought and conflict led to widespread hunger in Uganda.
- 1984 to 1985—Famine in Ethiopia. Drought in the northern highlands and problems delivering aid led to approximately 1 million deaths and massive displacements.
- 1991 to 1992—The Somalia famine was caused by drought and civil war.
- 1998 to 2004—During the Second Congo War, more than 3 million people died in the Democratic Republic of the Congo, mainly from starvation and disease.
- 2011 to 2012—The Horn of Africa hunger crisis was responsible for 285,000 deaths in East Africa.
- 2015 to 2016—A strong El Niño affected almost all of East and Southern Africa, causing food insecurity for more than 50 million people.
- 2017—25 million people, including 15 million children, need humanitarian assistance in East Africa. In September, inter-communal conflict in Ethiopia leads to more than 800,000 people being displaced internally.
- 2018—From February to May, torrential rains in East Africa caused floods that killed people, livestock, and crops, and washed away roads and bridges making it hard to deliver aid. In June, while rain will bring some relief to dry pastures and cropland, this is the height of the lean season; hunger is increasing.

Fast Facts: East Africa Hunger Crisis

Recurring failed rainy seasons have made it impossible for many East African farmers and herders to keep up their livelihoods. Flash floods during the 2018 rainy season are increasing humanitarian needs in South Sudan, Ethiopia, Somalia, and Kenya.

- 6 million people in the East African region are displaced due to conflict and drought, making them dependent on aid to meet their needs.
- Communicable diseases threaten the lives of children. More than 131,000 cases of acute watery diarrhea or cholera were reported in Ethiopia, Somalia, and Kenya during 2017, according to the World Health Organization. Measles outbreaks in Ethiopia and Somalia affected more than 24,000 children.
- Conflict, hunger, poverty, and displacement create a climate in which children are at risk of violence and exploitation.
- Help is necessary to keep the Africa hunger and food crises from worsening. Children, especially those younger than 5, are the most vulnerable because they need critical nutrients to build strength and immunity against disease.

Why Are People in Africa Facing Chronic Hunger?

Recurring drought, conflict, and instability have led to severe food shortages. Many countries have struggled with extreme poverty for decades, so they lack government and community support systems to help their struggling families.

A compressed cycle of recurring drought is plunging the same communities into drought again before they have a chance to recover sufficiently from the last one.

In South Sudan, where people fled their homes because of violence, few farmers have been able to harvest a crop. This limits what is available at community markets and raises food prices. In addition, during the rainy season, 60 percent of the country is inaccessible by roads, which limits transportation of food aid as well as goods sent to market.

From March through May 2018, long rains have been 150 to 200 percent above normal in some East Africa locations. This will bring some relief to herders as livestock benefit from renewed grasslands. However, in many places flash floods and overflowing rivers have wiped out crops, roads, and bridges, thwarting both cultivation and relief activities.

In such conditions, poor families can't afford enough food to keep their children healthy, and eventually, they need emergency help from government agencies or aid groups when they run out of money and food. We're not talking low funds or food that's been in our pantry that's well past its expiration. We're talking about not having any money or any food at all—nothing.

The longer these factors persist, the harder it is for families to stave off the effects of lost livelihoods and homes.

I Hear the Word Famine a Lot, but How Do You Define Famine?

The word *famine* means an extreme scarcity of food. But it's more than that—it's the absolute worst-case scenario for a food crisis and has a technical definition used by the humanitarian community.

Keep in mind that not all food crises become famines. A food crisis becomes a famine when there's so little food in the region that it causes large-scale starvation, malnutrition, and death.

South Sudan declared famine in February 2017 in two counties in Unity state with a population of about 100,000. By July, enough aid had reached the area so that famine conditions had ended.

To declare a famine, the following three things must all happen:

- At least 20 percent of households in a given area face extreme food shortages with limited ability to cope.
- More than 30 percent of children suffer from acute malnutrition.

- Hunger causes more than two deaths each day for every 10,000 people.

When a food crisis no longer meets these technical criteria, a famine is no longer in effect.

Why Does It Seem like There's Always a Hunger Crisis in Africa?

Drought, poor harvests, and instability create a cycle that's extremely difficult to break. And this happens in other regions of the world too.

When instability persists because of conflict or political problems, people flee their homes or are unable to plant their crops. Then less food gets harvested. Prices go up. Families' livelihood prospects dwindle as markets close. Violent conflict makes situations worse because humanitarian groups often cannot access affected communities to bring emergency relief.

Droughts have become more frequent and intense in recent years in western, eastern, and southern Africa. These droughts affect food-production systems in fragile contexts in similar ways that conflict does. Less food and water also means vast numbers of dead livestock in affected areas. This devastates families' source of income and food.

And when nearly 40 percent of children in sub-Saharan Africa grow up stunted due to chronic malnutrition, they lack the capacity to learn and contribute to society. It's because their little bodies don't get enough of the right nutrients at the right times to support physical and intellectual growth. Thus, their countries lose out on significant leadership and innovative potential, which perpetuates the cycle of poverty and deprivation.

What Is Malnutrition?

Malnutrition refers to an unhealthy condition that develops when your body does not get enough of the vitamins, minerals, and other nutrients it needs to function properly. It can occur when you don't eat enough food or you aren't eating enough healthy food.

When food crises happen, some children are malnourished for long periods. This leads to stunting (being underweight for their age). Children who were already growing poorly when the food crisis began now risk becoming permanently stunted (being short for their age).

Those who are most at risk experience severe acute malnutrition, known as severe wasting. This means their bodies are beginning to lose the ability to absorb vital nutrients. So they're literally starving to death. And they're nine times more likely to die than a well-nourished child.

Malnourished children don't just need more food. They need nutrient-rich food treatment, called ready-to-use therapeutic food (RUTF).

You've seen the photos—children getting their arms measured with the mid-upper arm circumference (MUAC) strips to gauge their level of malnutrition.

Medical workers often measure a child's mid-upper arm circumference to gauge the level of malnutrition the child is experiencing. That's why you may see photos of people wrapping a band with green, yellow, and red sections around a malnourished child's tiny upper arm. Green indicates the child is not malnourished. Yellow indicates malnourishment. Red indicates severe malnourishment and risk of death.

Malnutrition is the cause or a contributing factor to 45 percent of deaths among children younger than 5 globally, according to the World Health Organization.

How Is World Vision Responding to the East Africa Hunger and Food Crisis?

World Vision has scaled up efforts in Kenya, Ethiopia, Somalia, and South Sudan to reach up to 2.2 million people with life-saving food, clean water and sanitation services, medical assistance, and livelihood skills training.

Here are some highlights from our response in 2017:

- 2.4 million people reached with food-security and livelihoods support
- 2 million people reached with health and nutrition services
- 1.2 million people reached with water, sanitation, and hygiene services
- 145,000 children reached with protection and education activities

Funding provided through child sponsorship programs in Kenya and Ethiopia enabled our local staff to intervene to assist communities in 2016 before the crisis intensified. They provided drought-resistant seeds and training for farmers, cash-for-work programs, and other interventions that help families avert crisis or weather it more confidently.

By the time the food crisis became full-fledged, staff in South Sudan and Somalia were already helping communities struggling with food insecurity and malnutrition due to conflict and years of persistent drought.

How Can People Become Resilient So They Don't Need Aid?

There's no substitute for life-saving aid in an emergency. But World Vision also focuses on long-term solutions that build resilience, which allows families and communities to bounce back when crops fail or streams dry up. Livelihood skills training is one aspect of World Vision's current responses that help families find their own way out of a food crisis.

With long-term development programs in place, hunger crises can often be avoided and families can maintain independence. Here's how World Vision is working today to prevent future food and hunger crises:

- Farmers and pastoralists benefit from market development, immunizations for livestock, and training and seeds to grow drought-resistant crops.

- Cash aid gives impoverished families the ability to take care of themselves and stimulates local markets.
- Saving groups and community banks make loans that help members recover from emergencies.
- Building and repairing water and sanitation facilities contribute to healthy living.
- New business training, equipment, and materials can help families diversify their income so their assets are not wiped out by drought or adverse weather.
- Developing resilience is a generational process. Children who stay in school are better prepared for the challenges and opportunities in their future.

How Can I Help Hungry Children and Families in East Africa?

1. Pray for children and families affected by famine and hunger crises in East Africa.
2. Give to our East Africa hunger crisis fund. Your gift will help provide emergency food aid, agricultural support, clean water, medicine, and other essential care to hungry children and families.
3. Sponsor a child. World Vision's sponsorship program is the most powerful way you can help fight poverty at the family and community level. When you sponsor a child, you provide access to life-saving basics like nutritious food, healthcare, clean water, education, and more. You will help change a child's life story and the life of their family and community.

World Vision's Work to Combat Hunger in Africa

For more than 40 years, World Vision has brought emergency aid and long-term assistance to families and communities in East Africa.

Here are some of the ways we help to overcome the root causes of hunger and malnutrition in Africa:

- Food assistance, including emergency feeding and cash
- Diagnosis and treatment of childhood malnutrition
- Water and sanitation to prevent water-related diseases and provide water for irrigation
- Support for improved, more efficient agriculture and for farmers to diversify livelihoods
- Land rehabilitation to improve harvests

Viewpoint 4

From Arab Spring to Global Revolution

Paul Mason

In the following viewpoint, Paul Mason contends that the protest movement kicked off during the Arab Spring in 2011 would be permanent and global. His assertion is that social networking on a worldwide scale will continue to play a role in bringing protesters in various countries together for a common purpose, just as it did in Egypt and other Middle Eastern nations. Mason is a writer and broadcaster specializing in the subjects of economics and social justice.

As you read, consider the following questions:

1. What contentions does the author make in tying the Arab Spring to a larger global revolution?
2. In what ways does the author credit social media for greater citizen involvement in issues worldwide?
3. How does the author compare the current trend toward global citizenship positively to historical events in this article?

Two years on from the fall of Hosni Mubarak, the new Egyptian president is from the Muslim Brotherhood; on the streets of Cairo, the same kind of people who died in droves in 2011 are still getting killed. On the streets of Athens, the neo-Nazi party Golden Dawn is staging anti-migrant pogroms. In Russia, Pussy Riot are

"From Arab Spring to Global Revolution," by Paul Mason, Guardian News and Media Limited, February 5, 2013. Reprinted by permission.

in jail and the leaders of the democracy movement facing criminal indictments. The war in Syria is killing 200 people a day. It's an easy step from all this to the conclusion that 2011, the year it all kicked off, was a flash in the pan. But wrong. Something real and important was unleashed in 2011, and it has not yet gone away. I am confident enough now to call it a revolution. Some of its processes conform to the templates laid down in the revolutionary wave that swept Europe in 1848, but many do not: above all, the relationship between the physical and the mental, the political and the cultural, seem inverted.

There is a change in consciousness, the intuition that something big is possible; that a great change in the world's priorities is within people's grasp. The impervious nature of official politics—its inability to swerve even slightly towards the critique of capitalism intuitively felt by millions of people—has deepened the sense of alienation and mistrust.

But the changes in ideas, behaviour and expectations are running far ahead of changes in the physical world. There is greater space for democratic movements in the Arab world, but they are constantly menaced. "The Protester" may have made it on to the cover of *Time*—but not a single protest has yet achieved its aim.

If we take 1848–51 as a template, the crucial moments of reaction lie ahead: coups, crackdowns, intelligence-led disruption of the activists and hackers. But there is still one powerful factor militating against a return to stability of the kind achieved after 1848: the economy. Even if the Eurozone remains stabilised, and America avoids a political crisis over its budget, the developed world faces years of Japan-style stagnation.

In February 2011, in a blog titled Twenty Reasons Why It's Kicking Off Everywhere, I argued that there was a "new sociological type" at the heart of the global protests: "the graduate with no future." Since then *indignados* have flooded into Madrid's Puerta del Sol; Occupy camps have sprung up in hundreds of cities across the globe; and student protests in Chile and Quebec have completely changed the political atmosphere there. The anger is undimmed.

But the limits of what young protesters are prepared to do have become more obvious.

Free-market capitalism offered the generation born after 1985 the moon and stars. Now, in the west, it can offer very little. Even for those with jobs, there is a dramatic scaling back of opportunity that makes no version of the future seem palatable. In Athens, I interviewed a female anti-fascist, who alleged she had been strip-searched and abused in the police HQ: what was her job? "I wait tables," she said, adding with an embarrassed laugh, "but I am a qualified civil engineer."

To survive, the young have become a generation of drifters, reliving the plotlines of movies from the 1930s. Without some massive and cathartic turnaround, the generation in their 20s, in the west, will never accumulate pay, conditions or savings at the level their parents did. What they are accumulating is resentment.

In February 2011 I pointed to the use of social networks to organise protest, and argued that this had made "all propaganda flammable." Two years on there's a clearer pattern: the interaction of social media with a mainstream media that is, itself, undergoing rapid change. On protests you have started to see geeky men wandering around with a GoPro camera on a bike helmet, linked to a computer and a makeshift aerial, effectively live-streaming the action to niche blogs. But you also now have mainstream news networks live-streaming the protests, albeit sometimes from the safety of a rooftop or helicopter. Wherever the traditional media has the guts to do it, they can show the unedited truth about protests: who starts them, who escalates them, who behaves stupidly, who not.

On top of this, social media have grown more complex. Slowly, quietly, the mainstream media have become, for many involved in activism, politics and journalism itself, a secondary source of information, while social networks have become the primary source. This, in turn, speaks to the emergence of an undeclared dual power between the world of ideas and the world of official politics.

When the revolutions of 2011 began, horizontalism was the most obvious feature. But disengagement from ideology and structure was to play a major role in the defeat or failure of the progressive movements in 2012. In Egypt, once politics was reduced to a battle between the Muslim Brotherhood-led parliament and the remnants of the Scaf (the Supreme Council of Armed Forces), the weakness of Egyptian democratic and secular politics was exposed. Even after two years of riots, crises, scandals and crackdowns, Egypt has produced no large liberal or leftist party that is simultaneously against Islamism, and in favour of a rapid completion of the revolution. In the process of creating the National Salvation Front the opposition has had to re-order itself, with the traditional leadership types at the top, the youth at the bottom.

Egypt, in short, is the clearest example of the revenge of the hierarchy: the revenge of the 20th-century ideologies that globalist, secularist netizens had convinced themselves would expire of their own accord. And while there are many specifics to the Egyptian situation, 2012 closed with a foreboding that maybe the old forces—religion, fascism, Stalinist communism, militarism—could revive and conquer elsewhere.

Two years into the upheaval, the massive involvement of young, educated women in the protests remains one of its most salient features. There's been an obvious and predictable backlash: rapes and sexual assaults in Tahrir Square and in various Occupy camps. In India the gang rape of a female student sparked the launch a mass movement mobilising the educated youth.

Within the protest movements in the west there has also been the consistent problem of men assuming leadership, and dominating the discussion, even in forums where "consensus" and the various speaker "stacking" systems were supposed to prevent it.

In general, women have been able to organise to counteract such outright sexism. But the wider problem remains: if a movement has no demands, then how does it articulate what women's liberation consists of? How does it fit the issues raised by women's long-term and strategic oppression into the immediate social issues of the day? In the horizontalist movements, this problem has hardly begun to be addressed. At root—as, for example, the radical journalist Laurie Penny has observed—it is because feminism has achieved social mobility for some women, and even a symbolically liberated lifestyle, but at the price of a truce over the economic and social subjugation of all women.

If you take a wide-angle view of this dilemma—personal liberation replacing a struggle for general economic and social liberation—it's simply a subset of the overarching problem with the movements of 2011–12. Being a counter-culture—or even a "counter-power"—is a viable strategy only as long as the dominant cultures and powers are benign and stable.

With hindsight, late 2011 was the moment the sheen on horizontalism faded. In Spain, the leading voices within the *indignado* movement became frustrated by the obsession with "process." The tyranny of consensus and hostility to political demands sucked away their momentum. Some have now organised a party—Partido X—whose debut political broadcast on YouTube featured a man in a tie.

With Occupy Wall Street, critics point to an emergent self-obsession. "There is a danger. Don't fall in love with yourselves," Slavoj Zizek told the protesters in Zuccotti park. "What matters is the day after, when we will have to return to normal lives. Will there be any changes then?"

The journalist Thomas Frank excoriated Occupy for its self-obsession, its refusal to express demands, comparing its minimal achievements with those of the Tea Party. Frank called for a movement "whose core values arise not … from the need for protesters to find their voice, but rather from the everyday lives of working people."

However, both in the US and Spain, the occupiers did—once their ability to capture physical space was suppressed—attempt to move towards everyday life. By mid 2012, wherever you went in Spain, you could find movements of the working class and poor that had become infused with a 5% dose of horizontalist activism. In the US, when Superstorm Sandy devastated parts of New York and New Jersey in November 2012, overwhelming the federal emergency response services, Occupy activists surged into the breach, organising food kitchens, emergency power supplies, informal car ferry schemes and emergency shelters. Soon the hashtag #OccupySandy was trending.

When the history of this crisis is written, one of the most fascinating tasks will be to document the memes that flowed throughout it. It will not be easy: the digital human consciousness is playful. Thousands of jokes are made each day on Twitter consisting, for example, of fake book titles on some iconoclastic theme. It will not be enough to document what they were, but who made them; the speed at which the irony flowed; were people at work when they retweeted? Did the meme stay local, or did it go global?

From Tahrir to Puerta del Sol, the most important thing about the slogans, images and gestures is not what they said in isolation but what they expressed cumulatively: the woman who walked naked through the riot outside the Spanish parliament, holding a sign saying "peace"; the video of Loukanikos, the Greek riot dog, which went globally viral in the summer of 2011; the "No Pasaran" T-shirt worn by Pussy Riot member Nadezhda Tolokonnikova in the dock.

These were first of all signifiers of rejection: scorn not just for the elite world of yachts, diamond watches and bodyguards, but for the everyday world of corporate conformity. Through these signs and symbols, large parts of humanity were signalling their solidarity to one another; their belief that a kinder, more human system is possible; and that it would be born out of the chaotic, ironic, playful qualities of human life—not by pitting one cruel hierarchy against another.

And this is why all exhortations to "formulate demands," embrace structure, or turn to "everyday life" miss the point: the activists' unwillingness to engage is precisely what has allowed them, up to now, to disrupt the timetable of official politics.

Two years ago I identified the defining character of this protest generation as follows: "People have a better understanding of power. The activists have read their Chomsky and their Hardt-Negri, but the ideas therein have become mimetic. Young people believe the issues are no longer class and economics, but simply power: they are clever to the point of expertise in knowing how to mess up hierarchies and see the various 'revolutions' in their own lives as part of an 'exodus' from oppression, not—as previous generations did—as a 'diversion into the personal.'"

If I could list only one and not twenty reasons why it is still kicking off, it would be the rise of the networked individual colliding with the economic crisis. Something fundamental has happened—a shift in human consciousness and behaviour as momentous as that triggered by the arrival of mass consumption and mass culture in the 1900s.

I am drawn to Virginia Woolf's comment: "On or about December 1910 human character changed." She was referring to a revolution in social life and art, which made the literary tools and conventions of the Edwardian era "dead for us." The protesters have made the 20th century seem as alien and remote as the 19th century was to Woolf and her circle.

The change, as sociologist Manuel Castells argues, is one-off and irreversible, like electrification, and it will condition all politics going forward. So the challenge for traditional politics, right and left, religious and secular, is, as Castells argues, that the networked social movements actually reflect the reality of "everyday" or "normal" life better than the old hierarchical forms. Exhorting them to "turn to the masses" misses the point: economic crisis is forcing large numbers of people to adopt behaviours that were once deemed "lifestyle choices" (squatting, bartering, sofa-surfing, the grey economy). If Castells is correct, we can expect horizontalism to survive its first winter of discontent, and to resist simple absorption into the trade unions or the liberal and social-democratic parties.

Regional Citizenship in South America

Over the last fifteen years a far-reaching free movement regime has been implemented in South America, with the three largest regional organizations (MERCOSUR, CAN, and UNASUR) concretely debating proposals for a South American citizenship. MERCOSUR is probably the best known and is, with 260 million consumers, potentially a lucrative market that may profit from many countries having to diversify their export destination in light of recent US protectionism.

The idea for a common citizenship in the region is not completely new. As noted by Diego Acosta, "already in the 19th century the Hispano-American regional citizen had emerged as a legal figure between the national and the foreigner, often enjoying better treatment than foreigners in general as well as preferential access to nationality." This, in turn, can be traced back to the broader concept of *Hispanidad*, which is also still invoked by Spain to maintain strong nationality ties with its former colonies and which has been broadened to include the descendants of the (Sephardic) Jewish community that was expelled from Spain in the 15th century.

Not only is the concept of South American citizenship often likened to that of EU citizenship in terms of rights and eligible categories, but it has been suggested that South American citizenship may lead the way in allowing for the possibility to acquire regional South American citizenship for non-Latin Americans irrespective of first acquiring the nationality of a Latin American country. This is currently not possible in the EU, where access to European citizenship is still dependent on holding a Member State nationality.

South America seems an ideal test case to see how far the idea of regional citizenship can reach. Sharing a common language, religion and relatively stable borders since acquiring independence in the early 19th century, did Nobel Prize winner Octavio Paz not already write in the *Labyrinth of Solitude* that "even now, a century and a half [after gaining independence from Spain], no one can explain satisfactorily the 'national' differences between Argentineans and Uruguayans, Peruvians and Ecuadorians, Guatemalans and Mexicans?"

Still, Latin America has a long way to go and South American citizenship will likely face the same hindrances as EU citizenship in Europe.

"Free Movement in South America: Towards a South American Citizenship?" by Olivier Vonk, Future Citizen Institute, September 12, 2018.

Now the movements are at a turning point. Their "revolution" remains trapped at the phase of ideology, culture, political debate. The real changes desired by those who protest are still only achievable by those prepared to wield hierarchical power: be it Egyptian opposition leader Mohamed ElBaradei, President Obama or Greek leftist leader Alexis Tsipras, waiting nervously in the wings.

The radical youth do not disdain "ordinary" or "everyday" life, or the unwashed, uneducated masses; nor do they fear to go up against batons and even bullets: the Indian anti-rape protests are just the latest proof of this. What they disdain and fear are the politics of traditional power. In the process of overcoming this, they will probably be forced to engage with the things they despise: compromise, parliamentary politics, the art of the possible, political Islam, organised labour. The question then is: on whose terms, and with what politics?

Here, there is a parallel with the 1930s that is worth exploring. The first four years of the crisis, from 1929 to 1933, were not marked by effective mass resistance. That happened later. The early 1930s saw social disorientation, catastrophic policy choices, dysfunctional and autocratic governments and the rapid rise of the fascist right.

It was Hitler's rise to power in 1933 that focused minds, amid the fear that something similar could happen in France, Austria and Spain. At the same time, Roosevelt's New Deal signalled the possibility of a progressive government after all. The events of 1933–34 forced movements that had been socially weak, divided, heavy on rhetoric and self-obsessed, to, basically, get real. Fear was the key.

Although you can—as the anarchist slogan says—"live despite capitalism," you can't live "despite" fascism, genocidal racism, extreme sexual counter-revolution and war. As the gears of mainstream politics and economic crisis clash and grind above their heads, I would expect this realisation to be the guiding factor in where the movements that began in 2011 turn next.

In Latin America, Deep Inequalities Reduce the Power of Citizenship

Carlos Vilas

In the following viewpoint, Carlos Vilas laments the weakening level of citizenship and economic realities of those in Latin America, particularly the poor, based on job loss, working conditions, bankruptcies, and other factors. Vilas believes that the vast economic differences between rich and poor in Latin America and the Caribbean have lessened the power of the latter and contributed to less stability. Vilas is an Argentine political economist currently affiliated with the National Institute for Public Administration in Buenos Aires.

As you read, consider the following questions:

1. How do the issues facing the citizens of Latin America differ from those facing Americans and Europeans?
2. Are there similarities between income inequality in Latin America and the United States?
3. What if any suggestions does the author indicate to bridge the gap between rich and poor in that region of the world?

According to the most recent estimates of the UN's Economic Commission on Latin America and the Caribbean (ECLAC), there were 209 million Latin Americans living in poverty in 1994, up from 197 million in 1990, an increase of 6%. A decade

"Essay: Inequality and the Dismantling of Citizenship in Latin America," by Carlos Vilas, September 25, 2007. This piece was originally published in North American Congress on Latin America (NACLA), Reprinted by permission.

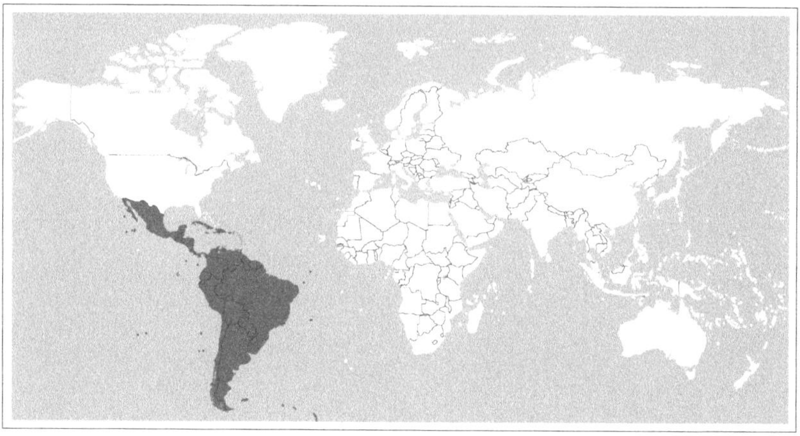

of neoliberal, market-oriented reforms had brought about the reactivation of private investment and economic growth together with an overwhelming deterioration of living standards and the impoverishment of large numbers of people.

Deep and persistent social inequalities have biased the nature of both economic growth and recession in Latin America. It is the poor who bear the brunt of recession through job loss, downgraded working conditions, falling real wages, small-business bankruptcies and so on. It is the wealthy, on the other hand, who are the first to benefit from growth through access to credit and foreign exchange as well as tax exemptions and other government benefits. In Argentina, for example, between 1990 and 1994, the so-called "golden years" of the convertibility program of Carlos Menem and Domingo Cavallo, GDP increased by one third—some $100 billion—and labor productivity grew by 50%. Real wages, however, remained virtually frozen and unemployment skyrocketed. By contrast, after the "tequila effect" of Mexico's December 1994 peso crisis rippled through Argentina, the country's GDP shrank by 4.6%, while unemployment almost doubled. In the Buenos Aires metropolitan area unemployment increased from 602,718 (12.1% of the labor force) in 1994 to 953,632 (18.8%) in 1995. The 1995 rate of female unemployment was even higher, 22.3%.[1] Both growth and recession, then, had clear class implications. Workers gained little during the boom and lost more than their employers during the crisis.

The highest levels of social inequality are found in Latin America, with 14 out of 17 countries ranking higher than much poorer countries in Asia and Africa. This income inequality has been a feature of the Latin American landscape well before the advent of neoliberal restructuring. In part this is because there is much more cumulative inequality in Latin America than in other regions. Different types of inequality, that is, stemming from class, gender, race, regional and even religious differences, tend to overlap, creating extremely rigid social structures.

This is particularly true in countries where class and ethnic domination combine, as in Brazil and Guatemala. And contrary to the neoliberal idea that "market-friendly" economic growth leads by itself to increased social homogeneity, we see that countries so divergent in size and rate of growth as Mexico, the Dominican Republic and Nicaragua have similar levels of inequality, as is also the case of Ecuador when compared to Argentina.

Nowhere is income polarization so extreme as in the four Latin American countries shown on the chart. Business elites in those four countries enjoy higher levels of income than many of their colleagues in much more developed countries. Argentina's CEOs, for example, earn 7% more than their US colleagues although Argentina's GDP per capita is one third that of the United States. Mexico's CEOs earn 12% more than those in France, while France's GDP per capita is nearly six times that of Mexico.[2] The region's persistently high levels of poverty and inequality pose some problems for the ongoing celebration of Latin American democracy. The current growth in poverty is taking place in countries that have regular elections and more or less open competition among political parties. These countries are governed by regimes that are considered to be democratic—for their regular elections and open competition—by the so-called "transitions-to-democracy" literature of the 1980s and by the "consolidating-democracy" discussion in the 1990s.[3] But even in the strictly political sphere, these approaches are clearly inadequate, and there is evidence that a number of "democratic transitions" have retreated to traditional caudillo politics or to regimes which combine democratic formalities with authoritarian rule.

I would like to suggest a different approach. In addition to open competitive elections, democracy requires the effective observance of the rule of law and the autonomy of the judicial from the executive branch of government. It also requires accountability of public officials, free access to information and the civilian control of military and security forces. In addition to these minimal political conditions, genuine democracy requires access to certain socioeconomic conditions such as education, jobs, health care and housing, which allow for the effective practice of citizenship. These conditions are sorely lacking in most of our "really existing" democracies.[4] Although electoral procedures and party competition may be found in settings of massive poverty and profound inequalities, poverty and inequality tend to distort the effective meanings of democracy and citizenship. In conditions of extreme poverty, formal citizenship may mask a retreat towards patron/client political relations, while democratic institutions frequently house authoritarian power relations. The tensions between inequality and impoverishment on the one hand, and democratic politics on the other, can have a devastating effect on the latter. This can be seen more clearly if we consider the question of citizenship.

Liberal democracy—the purported goal of Latin American political elites and their US supporters—can be thought of as the political regime of citizenship.

Citizenship, in turn, is made up of some basic, interrelated components including, minimally, the following: individual autonomy, involving personal freedom vis-a-vis all other individuals as well as individual freedom and rights vis-a-vis state power and power-holders; equality of rights and obligations of all individuals in a particular polity; efficacy, or the ability (and the perceived ability) to achieve desired outcomes through one's direct or indirect efforts; accountability, or the assumption of responsibility for one's deeds and their consequenses upon others (which must apply to public officials as well as to private individuals); empathy, or the ability to place oneself into settings and situations beyond one's locality or everyday horizon; and finally an idea or assumption of a shared belonging to something that is common to all citizens (the res publica, as the Romans called it, or the English commonwealth). These components of citizenship do not easily coexist with extreme and persistant inequality. Rather, they tend to get distorted in some of the following ways.

Autonomy. Personal autonomy refers to physical freedom as well as access to some basic resources that allow for a minimum of self determination: a decently paid job, education and access to information, sustainable living conditions, and the like.

Figures on income disparities suggest that while the elites have abundant and sometimes excessive access to such resources, increasing majorities of the Latin American population are deprived of them. There is certainly a great deal of freedom and autonomy among the richest 20% of the Brazilian households which collectively earn 67.5% of the country's national income, or among their colleagues in Guatemala getting 63% of the pie. They enjoy more than autonomy.

These elites, as the Brazilian sociologist Octavio Ianni put it, "behave not as rulers, but as conquerors." Quite the contrary in the lower floors of the social edifice: what kind of personal autonomy is experienced by the jobless, the homeless, the poorest 40% of the Latin American population getting 5.7% of their country's income in Mexico, or 5% in Venezuela, 7% in Brazil, 4.9% in Chile, 2.7% in Guatemala or 4.9% in Colombia?

The much-discussed crisis of political parties is in part the result of this immense social polarization.[5] The inability of political parties to process and respond to the demands and expectations of the impoverished without contesting the overall imprint of market-dominated restructuring reinforces people's alienation from conventional representative democratic institutions. Something similar can be said with regard to the increasing inability of unions to represent and mobilize the growing numbers of the un- and under-employed, and those expelled from formal labor markets because of transnational subcontracting, "flexibilization," and other forms of labor discipline.

In addition to their conventional political and economic objectives, most Latin American parties and unions traditionally performed a number of social-assistance functions with regard to jobs, education, health care and the like.

Because of neoliberal restructuring—including budget cuts and union busting—these social-welfare functions have largely disappeared. It is now the state, through "targeted" social policies, which directly fills the void left behind by the unions' and parties' retreat from the daily needs of their constituencies. Since state resources—compensating for the rigidities and shortcomings of the market—are not sufficient to reach the entire population in need, a poor-against-poor competition develops to get access to much needed resources.

Equality. In such polarized social settings, to speak of equality is plain mockery. There is, of course, a constitutional framework of legal equality, yet when socioeconomic and cultural disparities reach extreme levels, effective inequality tends to dominate legal equality. In these circumstances, the egalitarian democratic principle of "one person one vote" is devoid of any relevant meaning. In the upper levels of the social order it is quite obvious that "one person" has access to much more than one vote: we are dealing there with corporate power. Take the case of Carlos Slim, the wealthiest man in Mexico, whose estimated $6.1 billion of assets include controlling interest in the Mexican telephone giant Telmex as well as major shares of the nation's largest bank and most profitable financial firm.[6] Are Slim's political power and efficacy restricted to just the ballot he casts every two or three years? Hardly. On the lower levels, of course, "one person" does mean "one vote" although post-electoral pirouettes by government officers frequently empty voting of its ability to achieve the goals the majority of the electorate is pursuing; cheating "the sovereign people" looks like standard operating procedure in market-friendly democracies.

Efficacy. These inequalities in personal autonomy have a powerful impact upon efficacy. Patron/client relations of domination and subordination tend to substitute for relations among equals. Personal ties substitute for impersonal institutional loyalties. This is particularly clear on the lower rungs of the social ladder, and increasingly present among segments of the middle class. Having a friend or a relative who holds some powerful position tends to be more conducive to the achievement of specific goals—getting access to a health clinic or a job, having the roads paved, or garbage collected—than the entitlements granted by citizenship rights. The very vulnerability of people in poverty reinforces their search for someone else's efficacy, and personal relations take precedence over entitlements.

This is what the Mexican anthropologist Guillermo de la Pena calls "negotiated corporatism." Efficacy here refers to the ability of subordinate individuals to manage themselves in non-democratic power structures and social networks.[7] In a recent survey conducted in the Dominican Republic, for example, the demand for strongmen and for authoritarian solutions was most common in the most vulnerable segments of population: among lower-income respondents, among the less educated, among women more than among men and among blacks much more than among whites.[8] A direct, non-mediated political relationship tends then to develop between the impoverished masses and the power holders.

In this relationship, power becomes unrestricted, and the masses look for some basic security and the fantasy of a future. We have seen this develop in a number of countries. In Peru, for example, a vast majority of the most deprived population re-elected Alberto Fujimori in 1995, while in Brazil the poor opted for Fernando Collor de Mello in 1990, and for Fernando Henrique Cardoso in 1995.

In none of these cases was the successful candidate backed by full-fledged political parties nor by labor unions.

Loss of efficacy takes place in at least two interrelated senses or levels: with regard to one's individual ability to achieve personal goals, and with regard to politics as a way to cope with collective conflicts and troubles. There is then a frequent overlap of electoral support for strongmen or caudillo-type candidates, and electoral absenteeism. According to a nation-wide survey conducted at the Institute of Social Research of Mexico's National University (UNAM), 29% of the Mexicans interviewed never talk about politics. Political indifference, however, is higher among people with no schooling (52%), among elementary-school dropouts (49%) and among those in the lower economic strata (47%).[9] A similar disdain for politics has been found in surveys on political culture in both Nicaragua and El Salvador.[10] Consequently, high electoral absenteeism should come as no surprise: 60% in the Salvadoran congressional and municipal elections in March 1997 and 40% in the first round of the so-called "elections of the century" in 1994.

Mexico's very high electoral absenteeism, on the other hand, receded sharply in the July 1994 presidential elections when electoral competition grew, opposition parties gained more room for conducting their campaigns, international observers were allowed to watch over the polls, and there was a feeling among the public that the coming elections could bring a change in their lives. Electoral participation went up to more than 73%, a historical record.

Loss of political and social efficacy is neither a spontaneous nor a "natural" phenomenon. It is a dimension of political power, nurtured by escapist fare from most of the media networks, and neoliberal assistance programs like Mexico's once-celebrated PRONASOL which oscillate between repression and the cooptation of independent popular organizations. In this context, one of the key—and most difficult—steps of political organizing is the process of convincing people that their own efforts can be fruitful in putting an end to their daily suffering.

Accountability. In settings of perceived powerlessness, impunity substitutes for accountability.

The belief that there will be no punishment for violations of the law is not just a subjective or psychological feeling; it is nurtured by the objective evidence that there are no legal sanctions for lawbreaking. When impunity exists, it tends to permeate the entire social structure, even while manifesting itself in quite different forms: pervasive tax evasion particularly in the upper levels of business corporations; "flexible" labor relations that enable business firms to fire workers with neither advance notice nor compensation; drivers passing through red lights and bribing police officers; the omnipotence of bureaucrats; police brutality in their dealings with the poor and the political opposition; open or poorly hidden corruption at all levels of government administration.

Poverty. Poverty is usually accompanied by a feeling of powerlessness which in turn is reinforced by the objective insecurity pervading everyday life in poor neighborhoods. In this setting, voting may harbor quite a different meaning from that involved in conventional political theory. For most educated and concerned citizens voting may be associated with general proposals of how to run the country, what to do with foreign trade, how to manage the foreign debt, what strategy of poverty alleviation is best suited to the situation, and so on. As field research has found, this is not the case in the world of poverty. Here, voting is an ingredient of an overall system of tradeoffs between the haves and the have-nots, an instrument to achieve specific resources like schooling, jobs, personal security, land titles, and the like.[11] In this environment, the ballot becomes something like the credit card of the poor.

It would be misleading to conclude that authoritarianism lies deep in the hearts and minds of the poor. In the recent past the Latin American poor have been active participants in revolutionary struggles in Central America, as well as in democratization processes in South America and the Caribbean. It is the authoritarian nature of post-adjustment settings which, in the absence of viable and credible progressive alternatives, biases the options of the masses toward a variety of authoritarian options.[12] When there is no foreseeable long-run and inclusive alternative, people have no option but to seek immediate, short-run solutions, particularly when these solutions provide tomorrow's food or today's job.

Empathy. Under conditions of extreme inequality, empathy recedes to close direct affective ties: the family or kin group, locality, religious or ethnic groups. It becomes extremely difficult, if at all possible, for the poor to decipher landscapes beyond their daily lives and troubles and their immediate localities. A retreat to "primordial ties"—as anthropologist Clifford Geertz termed them—takes place which substitutes for the "imagined communities" of nation, state, or anything falling beyond the frontiers of everyday life.

Under the conditions of neoliberal restructuring, the processes and institutions that can foster a broader social empathy—education, accessible information, community-based organizations—are becoming smaller and less accessible.

Public education is shrinking due to privatization; shrinking public budgets are driving museums and libraries into complete disarray; and the "global superhighway" is out of the reach of people not having access to a home phone—not to speak of the cost of equipment. Cross-country mobility is curtailed by privatization of transportation, increasing fares and decreasing family income, and even state-sponsored "social tourism" is a phenomenon of the past due to cutbacks in social spending.

Shared Belonging. "Everyone for her or himself" now substitutes for the commitments to shared belonging to the polity. Huge and usually increasing social distances between the richest and the poorest conspire against solidarity. The commonwealth is no longer common: it has been privatized and belongs to the wealthiest. As the German political scientist Herman Heller stressed, the very idea of a shared code of meanings involving everyone in the polity usually retreats when confronted to structural inequality and exclusionary development.[13] Like empathy, shared belonging is learned through processes and institutions. It is hard for people expelled from formal education, from access to basic social resources such as health care, a decent house—even a decent room—because of joblessness and poverty, to feel members of the same social setting than those having them in excess.

In turn, allegiance to an international governing class and to the corporate world has replaced citizenship in the ranks of the very wealthy. Elites have loosened their material and symbolic links to any particular country, any particular polity or any particular citizenship, becoming increasingly committed to corporate interests and goals and even to the country that houses the headquarters of the corporations they work for. Democratic accountability has been eroded even further with the growth of the national elites' political accountability to the global financial community and to multilateral agencies like the International Monetary Fund (IMF), World Bank and the Inter-American Development Bank (IDB). Due to the politically conditioned support from these financial agencies, many government officials consider themselves no longer accountable to their citizens but to the lending agencies themselves. The relation of representation which is central to any electoral democracy has moved from a link between government and citizens, to a link between government and the financial institutions.

The self-empowerment of the people, moving from clientism to a full-fledged citizenship, is the only way out of these authoritarian democracies—the only escape from authoritarianism in general. Most of the agenda for the enlargement of effective democracy has been prompted by the efforts of people to organize themselves in the face of repression from governments and scorn from conservative intellectuals. From these efforts have come the movements for human rights, labor rights, freedom of information, women's rights, ethnic and racial pluralism, peasant access to land, the rule of law and environmental protection.

In its very beginnings, citizenship was accessible to just a tiny proportion of individuals—free, literate, adult, propertied, native-born males. It has been the task and the success of a whole range of social movements to open up the rights and obligations of citizenship to larger proportions of the adult population, emancipating both citizenship and democracy from class, gender and racial boundaries. Yet this move from subordination to citizenship is neither spontaneous nor inevitable. As with everything in politics—and in human life—it has to be brought about by need, desire, and commitment.

Notes

1. International Labor Organization, *Yearbook of Labor Statistics 1996* (Geneva: ILO, 1996), p. 389.
2. Research on CEO salaries conducted by the consulting firm Towers Perrin, Pagina 12 (Buenos Aires), February 16, 1997. GDP figures are from World Bank, *World Economic Report 1996* (Washington, D.C.: World Bank, 1996).
3. See Guillermo O'Donnell, "Illusions About Consolidation," *Journal of Democracy*, Vol. 7, No. 2, April 1996, pp. 34–51.
4. See Carlos M. Vilas, "Participation, Inequality, and the Whereabouts of Democracy," in D. Chalmers, C.M. Vilas, et al., eds., *The New Politics of Inequality in Latin America* (Oxford: Oxford University Press, 1997), pp. 3–42. See also Steven Volk, "'Democracy' Versus 'Democracy,'" *NACLA Report on the Americas*, Vol. XXX, No. 4, January/February 1997, pp. 6–12.
5. See Claus Offe, *Contradicciones en el estado de bienestar* (Madrid: Alianza, 1990), pp. 151–167.
6. See Carlos Marichal, "The Rapid Rise of the Neobanqueros," *NACLA Report on the Americas*, Vol. XXX, No. 6, May/June 1997, pp. 27–31.
7. Guillermo de la Pena, "Estructura e historia: La viabilidad de los nuevos sujetos," in *Transformaciones sociales y acciones colectivas* (Mexico City: El Colegio de Mexico, 1994), pp. 141–159.
8. Isis Duarte, et al., *La cultura politica de los dominicanos* (Santiago de los Caballeros: Pontificia Universidad Catolica Madre y Maestra, 1995).
9. Institute of Social Research/UNAM, *Los mexicanos de los noventas* (Mexico City: IIS/UNAM, 1996).
10. Mitchell Seligson, Political Culture in Nicaragua: Transitions 1991–1995, Monograph, Washington, D.C., December 1995; Jack Spence, et al., *Chapultepec Five Years Later: El Salvador's Political Reality and Uncertain Future* (Boston: Hemispheric Initiatives, 1997).
11. See Francisco Weffort, *Qual democracia?* (Sao Paulo: Schwarcz, 1992). See also Mercedes Gonzalez de la Rocha, *The Resources of Poverty: Women and Survival in a Mexican City* (Oxford: Basil Blackwell, 1994).
12. See a lengthy discussion of this point in Carlos M. Vilas, "Are There Left Alternatives? A Debate from Latin America," in Leo Panitch, ed., *The Socialist Register 1996* (London: Merlin Press, 1996), pp. 264–285.
13. Herman Heller, *Escritos politicos* (Madrid: Alianza, 1985), pp. 257–268.

Periodical and Internet Sources Bibliography

The following articles have been selected to supplement the diverse views presented in this chapter.

Bakersfield College, "Global Citizenship." http://www2.bakersfieldcollege.edu/gdumler/Engl%201A/X%20Research%20Papers/paper_two_global_citizenship_topics.htm.

Norma G. Finkelstein, "The Gaza Blockade Is Illegal—and So Is the Use of Force to Maintain It," Mondoweiss, July 7, 2018. https://mondoweiss.net/2018/07/blockade-illegal-maintain.

Global Citizen, "How Exactly Does Global Citizen Tackle the World's Giggest Problems?," February 21, 2018. https://www.globalcitizen.org/en/content/impact-global-citizen-summary.

Lori Hanson, "Global Citizenship, Global Health and the Internationalization of Curriculum: A Study of Transformative Potential," *Journal of Studies in International Education* 14, no. 1 (2010): 70–88.

Natalie Jesionka, "4 Ways to Become a Global Citizen Today," Muse. https://www.themuse.com/advice/4-ways-to-become-a-global-citizen-today.

Eric Liu, "Why There Is No Such Thing as Global Citizenship," *Atlantic*, August 14, 2012. https://www.theatlantic.com/national/archive/2012/08/why-theres-no-such-thing-as-global-citizenship/261128.

Klaus Schwab, "Global Corporate Citizenship," *Foreign Affairs*, January/February 2008. https://www.foreignaffairs.com/articles/2008-01-01/global-corporate-citizenship.

Robyn Scott, "Why Being a Global Citizen Is the Wrong Way to Change the World," Medium, September 4, 2017. https://medium.com/@robynscott/why-being-a-global-citizen-is-the-wrong-way-to-change-the-world.

GLOBAL VIEWPOINTS

Chapter 3

The Influence of the Internet on Global Citizenship

Viewpoint 1

Going Digital Can Help the World

Lee Watanabe Crockett

In the following viewpoint, Lee Watanabe Crockett seeks to define what a committed citizen should strive to be, based on the modern powers of the internet and ability of people around the world to communicate and not only think but also act globally. The hope is that people will find in those connections an opportunity to work together ethically, morally, and economically to improve lives around the world. Crockett is an author and speaker for the Global Digital Citizen Foundation, which works to educate and cultivate responsible citizenry in the new digital world.

As you read, consider the following questions:

1. Does the author adequately answer the question with which he begins this viewpoint?
2. What suggestions does the author make to maximize positive global citizenship?
3. Are the internet and social media strong enough as global communicators to change worldwide citizenship, or are the grips of governments too strong?

One of the questions we're asked most often is "what is a global digital citizen?" Being a global digital citizen is about more than just being a citizen of Earth. These are leaders, learners, and

"How to Nurture Global Digital Citizenship and Why It Matters to the World," by Lee Watanabe-Crockett, Global Digital Citizen Foundation, June 13, 2018. Reprinted by permission.

creators. It's a way of living well in a world that's changing fast, and showing others how to do the same. That's why we seek to nurture global digital citizenship in our learners and ourselves: because it *matters*.

Carl Sagan once defined an ideal citizenry as people "with minds wide awake and a basic understanding of how the world works." Fundamentally, global digital citizens are concerned with both *connection* and *contribution*. In other words, they know our technology plays a part in a much larger communal picture of respect and responsibility. A global digital citizen is a responsible and ethical citizen, leveraging technology to foster community on a global scale through connection and compassion.

With all this in mind, we're going to lead you to a thorough understanding of the global digital citizen, why the world needs them, and how you can nurture global digital citizenship in your learners in the best ways.

Two Citizens in One

When connected technology first started to appear in schools, educators quickly realized the need for guidelines for acceptable use. As a result, *digital citizenship* is a term that arose to describe how a person should behave in the online world. Policies and programs created around digital citizenship are primarily the content of an acceptable use policy. They're also usually enhanced with an educational component focusing heavily on protecting oneself from online predation and cyberbullying.

Global citizenship is a well-understood concept relating to how one participates in and contributes to the world as a whole. So what is global digital citizen and how do they relate?

Over the past few decades, we've experienced the creation, expansion and assimilation of the digital world. There was the digital world, which was accessible to a limited demographic, and the real world in which we all lived. Through the rapid expansion of wired and wireless data combined with the explosion of devices capable of connecting to this network, we now live in a new reality that contains both the digital and the real world. Today, digital connected technology is as much a part of our daily lives as the microwave and refrigerator, which are now also connected to the Internet.

As the digital world is part of our world, digital citizenship is now a component of global citizenship, and is in fact only one of the facets of global digital citizenship we discuss below. It does, however, have the capacity for tremendous impact on who we are as members of the global community.

A global citizen:

- sees the world as a community in which all people live and prosper together
- understands their actions contribute to the values of the entire planet
- concerns how we participate in and contribute to the entire world

A digital citizen:

- adheres to guidelines that govern the ethical and responsible use of technology
- acts responsibly in all relationships and interactions in the digital world

When we mix these two together, it's the perfect recipe for the global digital citizen. Global digital citizenship addresses how we participate and contribute in the blended physical and digital worlds, and how we can leverage the digital world to grow citizens in this new reality.

Tying the Digital and the Global Together

A global digital citizen also understands that we can govern technology for the benefit of both ourselves and others. It is a citizen that views the world as an interconnected community.

Additionally, they realize we simultaneously share technological and human experiences regardless of culture, status, or political/religious beliefs.

We ourselves like to define the best assets of the global digital citizen using five tenets. Let's examine why they're crucial concepts for educators to teach and for students to adopt. We also have resources to help you nurture global digital citizenship in your learners, which we'll discuss later.

These five tenets are the essence of what it means to be a great global digital citizen. If your goal is to nurture global digital citizenship in your children, this is the perfect place to begin. By using the examples and resources, you can move positively towards turning good digital students into great global digital citizens.

Personal Responsibility

Personal responsibility includes demonstrating how we manage ourselves in matters such as:

- personal finance
- ethical and moral boundaries
- personal health and wellness
- relationships of every kind, both online or offline

Why it's important: For the student, this kind of responsibility means taking ownership of their learning. Developing a sense of accountability for lifelong learning in our students prepares them for the workplace. These are places where they must often think and act independently and take initiatives on their own. Encouraging this in the classroom as early as possible can help students develop high-level critical thinking and problem solving abilities to assist them in every aspect of their lives.

Some ideas:

- Put students into various project management roles.
- Encourage them to set their own learning goals and milestones.

- Let them create and discuss their own essential questions.
- Lead students towards self- and peer-assessment techniques.
- Used flipped learning strategies to engage students to learn independently
- Welcome input on class activities and schedules.

Global Citizenship

The global digital citizen understands that technology has dissolved boundaries between all the world's people. We now communicate, collaborate, and celebrate across all levels of society. In short, we are now all global citizens.

Why it's important: Our students must realize, among other things, that we aren't isolated from each other anymore. A deep understanding of this new global interconnectedness can encourage them to be aware of the issues, traditions, values, and cultures of other citizens. This leads to cultivating understanding, acceptance, compassion, and humility.

Some ideas:

- Involve students in projects on sites like Kiva.org, Kickstarter, or Vittana.
- Foster international connections using Skype in the Classroom.
- Explore and discuss the Miniature Earth Project, and create something similar that relates to the school or community.

Digital Citizenship

Digital citizenship covers appropriate and exemplary behaviour in our online environments. It's about working towards making our transparent digital world safe for ourselves and others.

Why it's important: Just like with personal responsibility, this involves moving accountability for appropriate behaviour to our students. We teach them how to govern their behaviour, act in just and moral ways, and lead by good example in all online associations. In doing so they foster independence within themselves and hopefully light the way for others to do the same.

Some ideas:

- Take a survey to find out what your students know about good digital citizenship.
- Carefully implement BYOD programs—use our BYOD Guide to help you.
- Employ Digital Citizenship Agreements to help you form great guidelines.
- Explore digital citizenship resources from Common Sense Media.

Altruistic Service

Altruism is defined as "having a selfless concern for the well-being of others." The global digital citizen acknowledges that they share this world with many different people. These ideals apply to the people we know, but also those we don't know. It includes embracing the opportunity to exercise charity and goodwill for the benefit of others.

Why it's important: The practice of altruistic service provides opportunities for our students to create meaningful connections to the real world. It gives them the chance to reach out to others and do things that can make a person's experiences better or easier in everyday life. This in turn produces a sense of community and well-being for all.

Some ideas:

- Create fundraising campaigns and other charitable acts with your students.
- Students can volunteer abroad using organizations like Projects Abroad or ISV.

Yes, There Is Such a Thing as a Global Citizen

I am annoyed by an op-ed in last weekend's *Washington Post* entitled "There's No Such Thing as a Global Citizen." In it, Jakub Grygiel, who (ironically) teaches at the School of Advanced International Studies, misreads reality and the ongoing change in political culture in the United States. (Another irony: His essay was published on the very weekend when global citizens around the world were honoring the memory of Nelson Mandela as a global, not just national hero.)

Why am I annoyed? First, the data make clear that huge numbers of people do identify as global citizens. That identification does not counter but strengthens their identity as the citizen of a country. In the last wave of the World Value Surveys (2005–07), almost three out of ten respondents "strongly agreed" when asked "Do you see yourself as a world citizen?"

Citizens of the United States are particularly likely to identify as "supranational" as well as "national." That's a natural reaction to the reality of a global economy and an Internet-based global system—a world in which what China does about burning coal and Europe does about its economic woes matters for the quality of life and the creation of jobs in the United States—and in which many Americans recognize the often unintended consequences (consider the global financial crisis) of mistakes at home on lives abroad. Around the world, it's the young and better-educated who are systematically more likely to identify as global citizens.

Second, contrary to Grygiel's argument, global citizens are naturally and legitimately concerned with policies of their own countries. A new generation of global citizens in the US is sensibly focused on pushing to get the US house in order, for the sake of better lives at home and abroad. Whether it's migration, trade, climate, technology or farm policy, what's good policy for Americans is also likely to mean a more secure and just system for people elsewhere.

This is obvious in the case of the US reducing its own greenhouse gas pollution, reforming its own immigration system and supporting public funding of the basic science here that has led to health, medical, agricultural and communications technologies that have transformed lives everywhere.

"Yes, There Is Such a Thing as a Global Citizen. There Are Lots of Them," by Nancy Birdsall, Center for Global Development, December 9, 2013.

- Students can work in their own community with local businesses to gain work experience and contribute to the well-being of community business leaders.

Environmental Stewardship

This practice is all about common-sense values and an appreciation for the beauty and majesty that surrounds us every day. This facet of global digital citizenship encourages exploring how we can practice the conscientious use of Earth's resources.

Why it's important: Environmental stewardship encourages every student to take a positive stand on personal, local, regional, national, and international actions regarding the preservation of what is essentially our "environmental community." This facet of global digital citizenship reinforces the idea that we have one world that we all live on. It's vital that we respect it and take steps to ensure its beauty and longevity for all future generations.

Some ideas:

- Explore websites like Endangered Earth, EPA, and EarthDay .org for information and learning resources.
- Ensure a good recycling program is in place at your school.
- Create a fundraising campaign to support an environmental group or your local recycling center.
- Create a "clean and green" school challenge and invite other schools to participate in developing the most effective policies and activities.

Why Nurture Global Digital Citizenship?

This is the fundamental question, and it's a fair one. After all, why should we seek to nurture global digital citizenship in our schools?

Why is it so vitally important to the present and the future? How can knowing and practicing all this help?

If you could sum it all up in one phrase, you could perhaps call it a quest for *mindful leadership*. We can address this using the essence of the 5 Tenets above.

Personally, we face the daily possibility of online fraud, identity theft, and online bullying. We place our entire lives and their contents in the digital stratosphere willingly, and often without considering the consequences. The dangers of this are real. What is needed is people who will advocate and demonstrate the kind of self-governance that will keep us safe from harm both online and offline.

Globally, even as technologically intertwined as we are, there is also a level of disconnection in our lives. We are more connected than ever and yet often less tuned into others than ever. Global digital citizens see the need all diversity has to be recognized, honoured, and cherished for present and future generations. They also see the need for harmony and connection in a world transforming as rapidly as ours.

Digitally our Internet is unchecked and growing wild, which can be a potentially good or bad thing depending on how it is approached by the individual. Although we don't subscribe to the belief that the Web is a haven for cyber-criminals who can act in complete anonymity, the truth is online perils do exist just as they do in the real world. A global digital citizen sets an example to others on how to navigate these potential dangers safely and securely. A good helping of common sense goes a long way in this regard.

Altruistically we have more means to help others thanks to technology. Crowdfunding and crowdsourcing help us give back to local and global communities. Social media can become a support network for those of us who are in physical, mental, and emotional need. The global digital citizen can lead the way.

Environmentally we continue to face growing threats such as climate change, resource depletion, industrial pollution, digital pollution, and more. Global digital citizens seek to combat the biggest challenges to our environmental health, and foster solutions that work to the benefit of the entire planet.

Viewpoint 2

The Internet Has Great Potential to Impact Global Society

Manuel Castells

In the following excerpted viewpoint, Manuel Castells examines the potential and impact, both positive and negative, of the internet on global citizenship and the world in general. He offers here that the digital revolution translates into greater individual power and an opportunity for people throughout the globe to gain a higher level of personal autonomy against the power structures of their nations. Castells is Wallis Annenberg Chair Professor of Communication Technology and Society at the University of Southern California.

As you read, consider the following questions:

1. How does the author define autonomy and relate it to digital technology?
2. What are some of the strongest global impacts of the internet, according to the author?
3. Why does the author believe ignorance is the main reason many people are overwhelmed by the power of the internet?

The Internet is the decisive technology of the Information Age, as the electrical engine was the vector of technological transformation of the Industrial Age. This global network of computer networks, largely based nowadays on platforms of wireless communication, provides ubiquitous capacity of multimodal, interactive communication in chosen time, transcending space. The Internet is not really a new technology: its ancestor, the Arpanet, was first deployed in 1969 (Abbate 1999). But it was in the 1990s when it was privatized and released from the control of the US Department of Commerce that it diffused around the world at extraordinary speed: in 1996 the first survey of Internet users counted about 40 million; in 2013 they are over 2.5 billion, with China accounting for the largest number of Internet users. Furthermore, for some time the spread of the Internet was limited by the difficulty to lay out land-based telecommunications infrastructure in the emerging countries. This has changed with the explosion of wireless communication in the early twenty-first century. Indeed, in 1991, there were about 16 million subscribers of wireless devices in the world, in 2013 they are close to 7 billion (in a planet of 7.7 billion human beings). Counting on the family and village uses of mobile phones, and taking into consideration the limited use of these devices among children under five years of age, we can say that humankind is now almost entirely connected, albeit with great levels of inequality in the bandwidth as well as in the efficiency and price of the service.

At the heart of these communication networks the Internet ensures the production, distribution, and use of digitized information in all formats. According to the study published by Martin Hilbert in *Science* (Hilbert and López 2011), 95 percent of all information existing in the planet is digitized and most of it is accessible on the Internet and other computer networks.

The speed and scope of the transformation of our communication environment by Internet and wireless communication has triggered all kind of utopian and dystopian perceptions around the world.

As in all moments of major technological change, people, companies, and institutions feel the depth of the change, but they are often overwhelmed by it, out of sheer ignorance of its effects.

The media aggravate the distorted perception by dwelling into scary reports on the basis of anecdotal observation and biased commentary. If there is a topic in which social sciences, in their diversity, should contribute to the full understanding of the world in which we live, it is precisely the area that has come to be named in academia as Internet Studies. Because, in fact, academic research knows a great deal on the interaction between Internet and society, on the basis of methodologically rigorous empirical research conducted in a plurality of cultural and institutional contexts. Any process of major technological change generates its own mythology. In part because it comes into practice before scientists can assess its effects and implications, so there is always a gap between social change and its understanding. For instance, media often report that intense use of the Internet increases the risk of alienation, isolation, depression, and withdrawal from society. In fact, available evidence shows that there is either no relationship or a positive cumulative relationship between the Internet use and the intensity of sociability. We observe that, overall, the more sociable people are, the more they use the Internet. And the more they use the Internet, the more they increase their sociability online and offline, their civic engagement, and the intensity of family and friendship relationships, in all cultures—with the exception of a couple of early studies of the Internet in the 1990s, corrected by their authors later (Castells 2001; Castells et al. 2007; Rainie and Wellman 2012; Center for the Digital Future 2012 et al.).

Thus, the purpose of this chapter will be to summarize some of the key research findings on the social effects of the Internet relying on the evidence provided by some of the major institutions specialized in the social study of the Internet. More specifically, I will be using the data from the world at large: the World Internet Survey conducted by the Center for the Digital Future, University of Southern California; the reports of the British Computer Society (BCS), using data from the World Values Survey of the University of Michigan; the Nielsen reports for a variety of countries; and the annual reports from the International Telecommunications Union. For data on the United States, I have used the Pew American Life and Internet Project of the Pew Institute. For the United Kingdom, the Oxford Internet Survey from the Oxford Internet Institute, University of Oxford, as well as the Virtual Society Project from the Economic and Social Science Research Council. For Spain, the Project Internet Catalonia of the Internet Interdisciplinary Institute (IN3) of the Universitat Oberta de Catalunya (UOC); the various reports on the information society from Telefónica; and from the Orange Foundation. For Portugal, the Observatório de Sociedade da Informação e do Conhecimento (OSIC) in Lisbon. I would like to emphasize that most of the data in these reports converge toward similar trends. Thus I have selected for my analysis the findings that complement and reinforce each other, offering a consistent picture of the human experience on the Internet in spite of the human diversity.

Given the aim of this publication to reach a broad audience, I will not present in this text the data supporting the analysis presented here. Instead, I am referring the interested reader to the web sources of the research organizations mentioned above, as well as to selected bibliographic references discussing the empirical foundation of the social trends reported here.

Technologies of Freedom, the Network Society, and the Culture of Autonomy

In order to fully understand the effects of the Internet on society, we should remember that technology is material culture. It is produced in a social process in a given institutional environment on the basis of the ideas, values, interests, and knowledge of their producers, both their early producers and their subsequent producers. In this process we must include the users of the technology, who appropriate and adapt the technology rather than adopting it, and by so doing they modify it and produce it in an endless process of interaction between technological production and social use. So, to assess the relevance of Internet in society we must recall the specic characteristics of Internet as a technology. Then we must place it in the context of the transformation of the overall social structure, as well as in relationship to the culture characteristic of this social structure. Indeed, we live in a new social structure, the global network society, characterized by the rise of a new culture, the culture of autonomy.

Internet is a technology of freedom, in the terms coined by Ithiel de Sola Pool in 1973, coming from a libertarian culture, paradoxically financed by the Pentagon for the benefit of scientists, engineers, and their students, with no direct military application in mind (Castells 2001). The expansion of the Internet from the mid-1990s onward resulted from the combination of three main factors:

- The technological discovery of the World Wide Web by Tim Berners-Lee and his willingness to distribute the source code to improve it by the open-source contribution of a global community of users, in continuity with the openness of the TCP/IP Internet protocols. The web keeps running under the same principle of open source. And two-thirds of web servers are operated by Apache, an open-source server program.
- Institutional change in the management of the Internet, keeping it under the loose management of the global Internet community, privatizing it, and allowing both commercial uses and cooperative uses.
- Major changes in social structure, culture, and social behavior: networking as a prevalent organizational form; individuation as the main orientation of social behavior; and the culture of autonomy as the culture of the network society.

I will elaborate on these major trends.

Our society is a network society; that is, a society constructed around personal and organizational networks powered by digital networks and communicated by the Internet. And because networks are global and know no boundaries, the network society is a global network society. This historically specific social structure resulted from the interaction between the emerging technological paradigm based on the digital revolution and some major sociocultural changes. A primary dimension of these changes is what has been labeled the rise of the Me-centered society, or, in sociological terms, the process of individuation, the decline of community understood in terms of space, work, family, and ascription in general. This is not the end of community, and not the end of place-based interaction, but there is a shift toward the reconstruction of social relationships, including strong cultural and personal ties that could be considered a form of community, on the basis of individual interests, values, and projects.

The process of individuation is not just a matter of cultural evolution, it is materially produced by the new forms of organizing economic activities, and social and political life, as I analyzed in my trilogy on the Information Age (Castells 1996–2003). It is based on the transformation of space (metropolitan life), work and economic activity (rise of the networked enterprise and networked work processes), culture and communication (shift from mass communication based on mass media to mass self-communication based on the Internet); on the crisis of the patriarchal family, with increasing autonomy of its individual members; the substitution of media politics for mass party politics; and globalization as the selective networking of places and processes throughout the planet.

But individuation does not mean isolation, or even less the end of community. Sociability is reconstructed as networked individualism and community through a quest for like-minded individuals in a process that combines online interaction with offine interaction, cyberspace and the local space. Individuation is the key process in constituting subjects (individual or collective), networking is the organizational form constructed by these subjects; this is the network society, and the form of sociability is what Rainie and Wellman (2012) conceptualized as networked individualism. Network technologies are of course the medium for this new social structure and this new culture (Papacharissi 2010).

As stated above, academic research has established that the Internet does not isolate people, nor does it reduce their sociability; it actually increases sociability, as shown by myself in my studies in Catalonia (Castells 2007), Rainie and Wellman in the United States (2012), Cardoso in Portugal (2010), and the World Internet

Survey for the world at large (Center for the Digital Future 2012 et al.). Furthermore, a major study by Michael Willmott for the British Computer Society (Trajectory Partnership 2010) has shown a positive correlation, for individuals and for countries, between the frequency and intensity of the use of the Internet and the psychological indicators of personal happiness. He used global data for 35,000 people obtained from the World Wide Survey of the University of Michigan from 2005 to 2007. Controlling for other factors, the study showed that Internet use empowers people by increasing their feelings of security, personal freedom, and influence, all feelings that have a positive effect on happiness and personal well-being. The effect is particularly positive for people with lower income and who are less qualified, for people in the developing world, and for women. Age does not affect the positive relationship; it is significant for all ages. Why women? Because they are at the center of the network of their families, Internet helps them to organize their lives. Also, it helps them to overcome their isolation, particularly in patriarchal societies. The Internet also contributes to the rise of the culture of autonomy.

The key for the process of individuation is the construction of autonomy by social actors, who become subjects in the process. They do so by defining their specific projects in interaction with, but not submission to, the institutions of society. This is the case for a minority of individuals, but because of their capacity to lead and mobilize they introduce a new culture in every domain of social life: in work (entrepreneurship), in the media (the active audience), in the Internet (the creative user), in the market (the informed and proactive consumer), in education (students as informed critical thinkers, making possible the new frontier of e-learning and m-learning pedagogy), in health (the patient-centered health management system) in e-government (the informed, participatory citizen), in social movements (cultural change from the grassroots, as in feminism or environmentalism), and in politics (the independent-minded citizen able to participate in self-generated political networks).

There is increasing evidence of the direct relationship between the Internet and the rise of social autonomy. From 2002 to 2007 I directed in Catalonia one of the largest studies ever conducted in Europe on the Internet and society, based on 55,000 interviews, one-third of them face to face (IN3 2002–07). As part of this study, my collaborators and I compared the behavior of Internet users to non-Internet users in a sample of 3,000 people, representative of the population of Catalonia. Because in 2003 only about 40 percent of people were Internet users we could really compare the differences in social behavior for users and non-users, something that nowadays would be more difficult given the 79 percent penetration rate of the Internet in Catalonia. Although the data are relatively old, the findings are not, as more recent studies in other countries (particularly in Portugal) appear to confirm the observed trends. We constructed scales of autonomy in different dimensions. Only between 10 and 20 percent of the population, depending on dimensions, were in the high level of autonomy. But we focused on this active segment of the population to explore the role of the Internet in the construction of autonomy. Using factor analysis we identified six major types of autonomy based on projects of individuals according to their practices:

a) professional development
b) communicative autonomy
c) entrepreneurship
d) autonomy of the body
e) sociopolitical participation
f) personal, individual autonomy

These six types of autonomous practices were statistically independent among themselves. But each one of them correlated positively with Internet use in statistically significant terms, in a self-reinforcing loop (time sequence): the more one person was autonomous, the more she/he used the web, and the more she/he used the web, the more autonomous she/he became (Castells et al. 2007). This is a major empirical finding. Because if the dominant cultural trend in our society is the search for autonomy, and if the Internet powers this search, then we are moving toward a society of assertive individuals and cultural freedom, regardless of the barriers of rigid social organizations inherited from the Industrial Age. From this Internet-based culture of autonomy have emerged a new kind of sociability, networked sociability, and a new kind of sociopolitical practice, networked social movements and networked democracy. I will now turn to the analysis of these two fundamental trends at the source of current processes of social change worldwide.

[...]

Viewpoint 3

Social Media Can Help the Government-Citizen Relationship

James Toscano

In the following viewpoint, James Toscano argues that social media does not automatically strengthen relationships between governments and the citizens of the countries they represent and that the world of education has a responsibility to teach all involved the most productive means to use social media to improve those relationships. Toscano expresses a belief in the potential of social media but thinks that work must be done to maximize that potential. Toscano is vice president of public affairs at Tidewater Community College.

As you read, consider the following questions:

1. What does the author believe the obligation of educators entails to further a positive relationship between citizens and their governments?
2. Why does the author believe time is the enemy of academic study?
3. What arguments does the author make against social media playing a positive role in the relationship between people and their governments?

"Does Social Media Help the Government-Citizen Relationship? Depends Who You Ask," by James Toscano, The Conversation, 5/13/2016. https://theconversation.com/does-social-media-help-the-government-citizen-relationship-depends-who-you-ask-58481.

Depending where you live, maybe you follow your local transportation department on Twitter for construction updates. Or maybe you watch Periscope videos of city council sessions, or read live blogs of public school board meetings.

Around the world, governments and citizens are engaging on social media. For instance, the town government in Jun, Spain has famously ditched its traditional approach to municipal customer service and replaced it with Twitter interactions.

And Twitter extended the reach of emergency management agencies in the US Northeast after 2012's Hurricane Sandy, providing a "lifeline" to residents who needed critical information but lacked electrical power.

Two important US conferences took place on the same day earlier this spring on the subject of social media in government—one led by leading practitioners, the other by academics. Observers of each would have come away with drastically different ideas about social media's potential to improve the relationship between government and citizens.

People in the trenches—responding to citizen complaints on Facebook, or live-tweeting public meetings—are optimistic about how social media can influence government-constituent interactions. But some public policy experts within academia are much more sour about social media use by government.

Why would these two groups have such drastically different ideas about what's going on? As a scholar-practitioner who bridges these two worlds, I offer some insight.

"Losing Hope" from Within the Ivory Tower

On April 8, 2016, academics from a variety of schools, as well as a mix of practitioners from across Florida, gathered at the University of Central Florida's 10th Annual Public Administration Research Conference under the banner of "Social Governance: Developments in Digital Democracy." I attended and was a guest speaker.

The morning's keynote was delivered by Dr. Lori Brainard, associate professor of public policy and public administration at George Washington University. Her work focuses on how "government agencies use the Internet to activate and mobilize for change and to disseminate information, conduct transactions and engage in community building and collaboration."

Leaning on her own studies of local police, Brainard dampened the audience's enthusiasm for the potential of social media to positively transform the relationship between citizens and agencies. She pointed to "very little (that) suggests collaborative problem solving" in Yahoo discussion groups maintained by Washington, D.C.'s seven police districts in 2007. Her study of social media dialogue on Facebook, Twitter and YouTube in the top ten US police departments found similar results in 2011.

Brainard told the conference audience there was reason for those who are optimistic about social media—digital utopians, as she called them—to "lose hope." Her advice was that agencies should resist the pressure to join social media, and even pontificated about whether there was some "burnout" of social media taking place.

Practitioners Enthusiastically Full Steam Ahead

Meanwhile, on the same day but three time zones away in Reno, Nevada, the Government Social Media Conference (GSMCON) was underway. GSMCON is the leading gathering for government practitioners of social media and earns the monetary support of the big-time corporate social media platforms and software providers.

No social media gloom and doom would be found in this assembly.

In fact, the example of local police was held up as a shining illustration of how social media can positively transform their relationship with citizens. Take Nextdoor.com. This neighborhood-based social network, increasingly popular with law enforcement, allows for an exchange of information between concerned residents and local police. Tips can lead to arrests and police look responsive, improving neighborhood safety. The company recently piloted a polling feature with the Austin Police Department that allowed

The Internet's Influence on Democracy

The way we learn to use the Internet in the next few years will influence the way our grandchildren govern themselves. Yet only a tiny fraction of the news stories about the impact of the Net focus attention on the ways communication technology might be changing democracy.

Democracy is not just about voting for our leaders. Democracy is about citizens who have the information and freedom of communication they need to govern themselves. Although it would be illogical to say that the printing press created modern democratic nation-states, it would have been impossible to conceive, foment, or implement self-government without the widespread literacy made possible by printing technology. The more we know about the kind of literacy citizens are granted by the Internet, the better our chances of using that literacy to strengthen democracy. What good is health and wealth and great personal home entertainment media without liberty?

Every communication technology alters governance and political processes. Candidates and issues are packaged and sold on television by the very same professionals who package and sell other commodities. In the age of mass media, the amount of money a candidate can spend on television advertising is the single most important influence on the electoral success. Now that the Internet has transformed every desktop into a printing press, broadcasting station, and place of assembly, will enough people learn to make use of this potential? Or will our lack of news, information, and understanding of the Net as a political tool prove insufficient against the centralization of capital, power, and knowledge that modern media also make possible?

The same tool that affords tremendous power to the grassroots, the broad citizenry, the cacaphony of competing "factions" necessary for healthy democracy, also affords tremendous power to the elites who already have wealth and power. Guess who can best afford to apply the tool to further their ends? What's in it for big media interests to inform us about how we can compete with big media interests?

The political power afforded to citizens by the Web is not a technology issue. Technology makes a great democratization of publishing, journalism, public discourse possible, but does not determine whether or not that potential will be realized.

"How Will the Internet Influence Democracy?" by Howard Rheingold, Edge Foundation.

them to survey residents on safety issues; 2,400 users participated, leaving hundreds of replies.

No platform is perfect, and critiques do arise. But the bottom line is that law enforcement is taking advantage of new opportunities to interact with the community via social media.

GSMCON conference advisor Jay Socol, Communications Director for the City of College Station, Texas, told me public agencies should be on social media if at all possible. Citing his city's efforts to live-blog council meetings and share municipal presentations, Socol said

> Citizens feel we're much more accessible now because they are talking to/about us in social spaces—and are getting responses. Further, our organization, in particular, is much more transparent in that our information reaches thousands, thanks to social platforms.

Socol says social media enables citizens to engage with government from their home, workplace—anywhere they're carrying their mobile device—and he's convinced these interactions will improve in time. What practitioners like Socol realize is this: no matter the shortcomings of social media, the obstacles that have served to separate citizens and government in traditional public engagement remain. Getting citizens to show up at ordinary public meetings hasn't gotten any easier, and there's no sign of a coming rebirth.

The strategists who actually engage with citizens via social media are excited about whatever progress they do see between government and governed. But those who study this sort of thing can be pessimistic. Why the disconnect?

Two Views on the Same Landscape

Empirical studies popular in the academy encourage tightly focused research questions and methods so that reliable answers follow. The classic problem, of course, is taking those neat little answers and generalizing them.

Public policy professor Brainard's findings are what they are: narrow. What she found taking place in Yahoo! discussion groups in 2007, a platform long out of vogue, has little relevance for social media strategists today. In 2016, it's impossible to have a meaningful dialogue about police engagement with citizens on social media without consideration of Nextdoor.

Time is an enemy of quality academic study. Theories fade. Hot topics go stale. The problem is particularly acute when studying social media, as it is a highly dynamic field. Usage patterns change rapidly, and new platforms emerge each year seeking to displace competitors or carve out their own space.

While Brainard was talking Yahoo! discussion groups, Socol was telling me how he's considering whether the city of College Station should begin engaging with younger citizens on Snapchat—which didn't even exist during the periods Brainard studied.

It's not uncommon to find quantitative academic studies of what was known as "the big three": Facebook, Twitter and YouTube. But social media use is increasingly diversified, particularly with younger users; attempts to understand social media through the big three are limited. We are in a period of social media whack-a-mole. The minute you think you've got it all nailed down, another platform pops up.

Academics studying social media should take note: the platforms aren't what you thought they were by the time you've actually published.

I'm not surprised quantitative research of social media engagement between citizens and government finds there's much room for improvement. As my own social media research shows, policies, organizational practices, structure and beliefs bias organizations against social media, even those that use it. Rules that govern the use of federal funds in local community projects, for example, specifically direct agencies toward good old-fashioned public meetings and the use of postal mail. These regulations make no mention of email, social media or other modern modes of communication. Local ordinances are no better. It's no wonder that social media can be undervalued.

Practitioners are facing an uphill climb and not all are upbeat. Some who encounter a lack of understanding—or outright resistance—at the top may be shy in their approach to citizens on social media. And some more senior practitioners would rather delegate responsibility to a young whippersnapper than immerse themselves in these engagement strategies.

Time and again, government and industry have turned to the academy to solve important public problems. But when it comes to social media, unless we can produce more timeless work—work that can survive technological change so frequent it's almost constant—the academy runs the risk of being confined to the wings in public conversations that influence the future use of social media. Practitioners continue to push against the tide of organizational bias to deliver on the promise of social media to improve citizen-government engagement—no matter what academics might pontificate.

Viewpoint 4

Youth Who Use the Internet Are More Likely to Engage in Civic and Political Issues

John D. and Catherine T. MacArthur Foundation

In the following viewpoint, the John D. and Catherine T. MacArthur Foundation delves into the positive aspects of social media to create change. Citing the findings of a study that reveal the desire of young people to learn more about issues and gain greater involvement through the internet and social media, the authors argue that young people should be given far more credit than they have received for their motivations relating to social media. The John D. and Catherine T. MacArthur Foundation works to build social networks that lead to a fairer and more peaceful world. Its goal is to tackle humanitarian and global challenges such as overincarceration, climate change, and the threat of nuclear war.

"Does the Internet Make for More Engaged Citizens?" John D. and Catherine T. MacArthur Foundation, February 23, 2011. Reprinted by permission.

As you read, consider the following questions:

1. Does the viewpoint indicate that most people have underrated youths regarding their interest in world affairs?
2. How does the viewpoint indicate the internet and social media have inspired young people to become more involved citizens?
3. Do you believe that unbiased and purely factual news can be found on the internet, or must one find other sources as well?

Youth who pursue their interests on the Internet are more likely to be engaged in civic and political issues, according to a new study of student Internet usage by a group of civic learning scholars. Youth who use the Internet are also more likely to be exposed to diverse political viewpoints, the study shows.

The study's findings run counter to two commonly held assumptions: first, that the Internet makes exposure to divergent political viewpoints unlikely, the so-called "echo chamber" effect; and second, that the Internet promotes shallow activism among youth, so-called "slacktivism."

The first-of-its-kind longitudinal study by civic learning scholars of high school students' Internet use and civic engagement found that:

> For many youth, their interest in the Internet translates into engagement with civic and political issues. Contrary to popular belief, it is rare for individuals on the Internet to only be exposed to political perspectives with which they agree, but many youth are not exposed to political perspectives at all. Teaching new media literacies such as credibility assessment is essential for 21st century citizenship.

The study results are being announced by a newly-formed research network of scholars, Youth and Participatory Politics, that will build on the study results and launch further investigations into the ways in which the Internet and digital media are impacting democratic and political engagement, particularly among youth. The formation of the Youth and Participatory Politics (YPP) research network and the announcement of the study's findings come in the wake of numerous high-profile uprisings in North Africa and the Middle East in which digital media, the Internet, and social networking appear to have played a role.

"Youth participate via new media in countless ways. Those habits and skills appear to have been key supports in these protests," said Mills College education professor Joe Kahne, the author of the study. "Both in the US and abroad, so much civic and political life is online. We've got to pay attention to new media when we think about civic learning.

"Research demonstrates that many youth are disengaged from traditional forms of civic and political life but are very engaged with new media," Kahne said. "Our study findings strongly suggest is that there are ways to build on their engagement with digital media to foster engagement in civic life."

First-of-Its-Kind Study on Youth and the Internet

The study is unique, tracking hundreds of students over time and asking about online practices and civic and political engagement. Overall, more than 2,500 youth were surveyed and more than 400 youth were followed for several years. The participants came from a highly diverse set of 19 school districts throughout California. "We followed the same youth for up to 3.5 years. We assessed whether particular kinds of online activities were associated with increased or decreased youth civic and political activity," Kahne said.

The study, which was supported by both MacArthur and the Center for Information and Research on Civic Learning, examined three types of behavior: politically-driven online participation, online exposure to diverse perspectives, and interest-driven online participation.

"This study reveals how participatory political practices among youth are upending our uninformed assumptions," said David Theo

Goldberg, director of the system-wide University of California Humanities Research Institute and co-director of the Digital Media and Learning Research Hub at UC Irvine. The Youth and Participatory Politics research network is one of three major new research initiatives of the Digital Media and Learning Research Hub, which is part of the UC Humanities Research Institute.

The study examined, for example, how often students:

- Used blogs or social networking sites to share or discuss perspectives on social and political issues;
- Used the Internet to get information about political or social issues;
- Used email to communicate with others who are working on a political or social issue.

The students self-reported their answers to questions on digital media literacy and exposure to political diversity by indicating how much they agreed or disagreed with statements such as:

(a) I've gotten new perspectives on societal issues because of my online activities.

(b) I've had online conversations with people who have different values or political views than I do.

(c) I've been able to connect with people who care about the same things that I do through the Internet.

(d) I've been able to connect with people who share my views about ways to create a better world through the Internet.

To assess the access, effectiveness and potential value of digital media literacy programs, students were asked how frequently in their classes they:

(a) Had learned how to assess the trustworthiness of online information;

(b) Were required to use the Internet to get information about political or social issues;

(c) Were required to use the Internet to find different points of view about political or social issues;

(d) Were given an assignment where they had to create something to put on the Web.

Findings Contradict Conventional Wisdom

A comprehensive analysis of the students' responses found that:

- Spending time in online communities appears to promote engagement with society. Many worry that youth who spend significant time on fan sites or in online communities tied to hobbies, sports or other interests will become socially isolated. The study found the opposite to be true. Youth engagement in interest-driven online communities was associated with increased volunteer and charity work and in increased work with others on community issues. The Internet can serve as a gateway to online and offline civic and political engagement, including volunteerism, community problem-solving, and protest activity.
- More youth are in empty chambers than echo chambers. Individuals tend either to see many differing perspectives or none. Few youth, 5%, reported being exposed only to political views they agreed with. However, 34% of youth said that they didn't encounter any perspectives at all. "Many youth are largely disengaged from discussions and debates surrounding civic and political issues," Kahne said.
- Many think of youth as knowing all they need to know about the Internet and that adults have little or no role to play, but youth are not all "digital natives." The study found that digital media literacy education dramatically increased students' exposure to diverse perspectives and boosted the likelihood of youth online engagement with civic and political issues. This finding has serious implications for school and after-school programs as well as for parents. Many young people will benefit if they learn how to tap the full potential of digital media.

"We found that being part of online participatory communities tied to youth interests, political or not, exposes youth to a greater degree of diverse viewpoints and issues and is related to higher levels of civic engagement," Kahne said. "Both of these outcomes are good for democracy."

New Research Network to Expand Probe of the Internet and Democracy

Chaired by Kahne, the new research network on Youth and Participatory Politics will conduct national surveys and launch in-depth qualitative studies of the relationship between digital media, youth and political engagement. It will focus on the potential of digital media to inform and empower youth and foster constructive collective action and social enterprise both in the US and internationally. It will also examine ways to guard against the problematic dynamics associated with digital media, including the spread of misinformation, and the relationship between anonymity, responsibility and ethics.

"It's hard to imagine a more pressing issue than the next generations' involvement in our democracy," said Connie M. Yowell, director of education programs for the MacArthur Foundation in the US. MacArthur supported the civic engagement survey and study and is supporting the Youth and Participatory Politics research network as part of its Digital Media and Learning initiative. "Social media has clearly altered the nature of participation with implications for the economy, learning, and as we are now witnessing almost daily—civil society—both in the United States and globally," Yowell said.

"The Youth and Participatory Politics Network is an extraordinarily diverse group of scholars and practitioners," Yowell said, "who will bring both a fresh perspective and new evidence to the question of democratic participation in the 21st century."

The YPP's seven scholars bring collective insight from the domains of political theory, citizen media, ethics, participatory culture, social movements, education and interest-based learning:

- Danielle Allen, political theorist who has published broadly on democratic theory, political sociology, and the history of political thought, Institute for Advanced Study;
- Cathy J. Cohen, expert in American politics, African-American politics, women and politics, lesbian and gay politics, and social movements, University of Chicago;
- Howard Gardner, one of the world's leading experts and writers on intelligence, creativity, leadership, and ethics, Harvard University;
- Mizuko "Mimi" Ito, cultural anthropologist with deep expertise in the implications of how youth are engaging with technology and digital media, University of California, Irvine;
- Henry Jenkins, expert on new media and participatory culture, University of Southern California;
- Joseph Kahne, YPP Chair, expert on how school and new media practices influence youth civic and political development, Mills College;
- Ethan Zuckerman, co-founder of an international force of citizen bloggers called Global Voices, leading scholar on the Internet and democratic engagement, Berkman Center for the Internet and Society, Harvard University, and MIT Media Lab.

The MacArthur Foundation launched its Digital Media and Learning initiative in 2006 to explore how digital media are changing the way young people learn, play, socialize and participate in civic life in the 21st century.

"At a time when social media are transforming how youth engage with each other, with adults, and with the world more largely, the YPP research network is leading the way in understanding the changes in youth participation in politics, and the extraordinary possibilities and challenges that follow," said director Goldberg from the Humanities Research Institute. "I can't wait to see further results from the network."

Viewpoint 5

In China, Blogging Is Both Connecting and Not Connecting Citizens

James Leibold

In the following excerpted viewpoint, James Leibold examines the subject of blogging in China, a country that has become open to a more capitalistic economy but has not grown as a bastion of freedom of speech. Based on what he has read, Leibold is not optimistic that bloggers in China will be free to use their powers of expression to further the cause of freedom of expression in what remains the most populous nation in the world—even though it boasted nearly 200 million bloggers at the time he wrote this viewpoint. Leibold is a senior lecturer and Asian Studies program convenor in the School of Humanities and Social Studies at La Trobe University in Australia.

As you read, consider the following questions:

1. What does the author's contention that Chinese bloggers have not felt free to write critical opinions say about the country in which they live?
2. Does the author express any optimism about freedom of speech becoming a reality in China?
3. Can the internet make a positive impact on the cause of freedom in China, or does the Chinese government have a stranglehold on the people, according to the viewpoint?

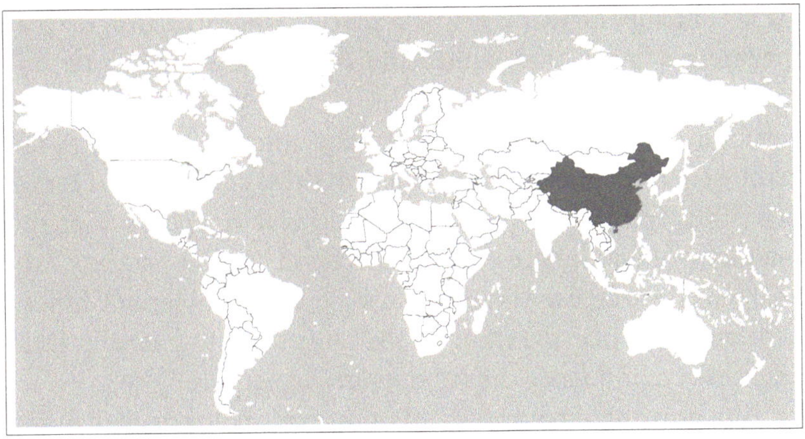

With 457 million users today and an estimated 650 million by 2015, the Sinophone internet is now the world's largest cyber-community, where netizens spend 44 percent of their free time (CNNIC 2011; TNS 2008). Despite the growing literature and hype surrounding the global "blogging revolution," China's 181 million bloggers have attracted little attention compared to their counterparts in North America and now the Arab world. This is despite the fact that there are now nearly three times as many active blog sites in China (329 million in 2009) as the 133 million largely English-language blogs indexed by the US-based monitoring service Technorati since 2002 (CNNIC 2009; Winn 2009).

More to the point, academic analysis of the internet in China has become bogged down in the ubiquitous yet increasing stale debate between digital-activism and cyber-censorship—the good versus evil struggle between the internet's liberating potential and the Chinese party-state's ongoing efforts at thought-control. Underpinned by the circular logic of technological determinism, this debate impedes us from asking equally interesting and far more complex questions about how online information and technologies are re-constituting Chinese society and identity. By moving beyond the information control/resistance paradigm, we can begin to explore how a range of different actors are deploying these new social spaces and informational flows to reshape public and private life in contemporary China. China watchers now tend to agree that the internet has both expanded and altered the discursive terrain of the People's Republic of China (PRC) while allowing its citizens to mobilize in new ways. What remains unclear, however, is the precise socio-political consequences of these changes. Positioned here, this Trends article presents a critical re-appraisal of the interactive blogosphere and its effects on Chinese society. My analysis is one focused on the discourse and behavior of Chinese netizens rather than the efforts of the Chinese party-state or private enterprise to influence their thoughts and actions.

The growing convergence of online technologies makes any differentiation based on functionality increasingly problematic, with individual sites now embedding multimedia, search, e-commerce, social networking, and blog features. In their special issue on the blogosphere, Daniel Drezner and Henry Farrell (2008, 2) provide the following definition of web-based blogs or weblogs: "a web page with minimal to no external editing, providing on-line commentary, periodically updated and presented in reverse chronological order, with hyperlinks to other online sources." This definition is broad enough to incorporate the different functionalities and uses of two distinct yet related types of user generation content in Chinese cyberspace: personal blogs or microblogs and community-based web forums (known as bulletin board systems, BBS). Both mediums provide a dynamic platform for asynchronous, interactive information sharing and discussion on a wide variety of topics. Taken together weblogs represent the single largest, and most dynamic, communication platform on the Chinese internet, providing unprecedented opportunities for netizens to both engage in national-level debate and indulge their personal fetishes in isolated, interest-based enclaves.

To date, analysts writing in English have painted a generally rosy assessment of the impact of the blogosphere on Chinese society. These range from those who speak of a "communication revolution" (Yang 2009, 213), "political liberalization" (Zheng 2007, 167), or a "gradual, slow evolution" (MacKinnon 2008, 45).

Others posit that the Chinese internet is "a platform for bottom-up information and public debate" (Zhou 2009, 1006) and "a new channel for individual expression" (Shen et al. 2009, 470), which either "democratizes communication of information in Chinese society" (Tai 2006, 289), "promote[s] political openness, transparency, and accountability" (Zheng 2007, 186), "erode[s] the CCP's ideological and social control" (Xiao 2011, 223) or "challenges the mainstream culture" through its "playful (mis) use (and often juxtaposition) of the available resources" (Yu 2007, 429). Playing on one of Chairman Mao's famous revolutionary phrases, Pulitzer-Prize-winning columnist Nicholas Kristof (2006) declared that a "single blog can start a prairie fire," arguing that the unprecedented free speech in the Chinese blogosphere threatens to eventually topple the Chinese Communist Party (CCP) from power. Even the euphemistic "harmonizing," or forced closure, of Kristof's own Chinese-language blog on Sina.com failed to dampen his confidence, when he boldly announced this year: "the internet will one day be remembered as helping to transform China, byte by byte. Let a billion blogs bloom" (Kristof 2011).

In sharp contrast, research and debate on the political impact of the internet in the West has been more robust and wide-ranging in its focus, and far more cautious in its conclusions. Many commentators continue to defend the innately empowering nature of new communication technologies, as first sketched out by Alvin Toffler and others in their 1994 manifesto "Cyberspace and the American Dream" (Dyson et al. 1996; see also Negroponte 1996; Benkler 2006; Shirky 2008). Yet, new empirical evidence and theoretical intervention have complicated this picture. In *The Myth of Digital Democracy*, Matthew Hindman (2008) demonstrates how blogging remains a narrow, elite pursuit, which does little to increase the representative basis of American politics, while Cass Sunstein (2007) has shown how blogging can actually fragment and polarize speech communities. Evgeny Morozov's provocative new book *The Net Delusion* provides a forceful critique of the naïve assumption that Google, Facebook and Twitter will bring down authoritarian regimes like China with a few clicks of the mouse, suggesting that in many authoritarian countries the internet actually "empowers the strong and disempowers the weak" (Morozov 2011, xvii). Recent events in the Arab world and corresponding calls for a similar "Jasmine Revolution" in China have intensified the debate (Coll 2011; Wasserstrom 2011).

But beyond the well-developed literature on internet censorship in China (see for example, Tsui 2003; Lagerkvist 2006; MacKinnon 2009; Jiang 2010), few studies have fully probed those elements of Chinese cyberculture that might be working against positive social change. Like other technologies, the internet is normatively neutral and socially malleable and, depending on the particular context and pre-existing social patterns, can function as a force for both good and evil. While any definitive assessment of the Chinese blogosphere awaits more detailed, empirical research, I will argue that much of the optimism that pervades current writing on the Chinese internet seems premature and possibly misplaced. Drawing on surveys of online usage, comparative research and my own personal engagement with the Chinese internet, this article suggests that the Chinese-language blogosphere is producing the same sort of shallow infotainment, pernicious misinformation, and interest-based ghettos that it creates elsewhere in the world.

Blogging isn't the same as bowling. And clearly holds the potential to link individuals and communities in revolutionary new ways—counteracting the worldwide decline in civic engagement identified by Robert Putman (2000) and other sociologists. But before declaring that the Sinophone internet and weblogs are "changing the rules of the game between society and the state" and contributing to an unprecedented "power shift in Chinese society" (Xiao 2011, 203, 222), we need to explore the complex and countervailing ways that sitting alone in front of our blinking screens can both connect and disconnect us from others; alter and perpetuate long-standing patterns of socio-political engagement.

Periodical and Internet Sources Bibliography

The following articles have been selected to supplement the diverse views presented in this chapter.

BBC, "Social Media and Censorship in China: How Is It Different to the West?," September 26, 2017. http://www.bbc.co.uk/newsbeat/article/41398423/social-media-and-censorship-in-china-how-is-it-different-to-the-west.

Global Citizen, "Social Media: A Triumph or Tragedy?," April 24, 2018. https://medium.com/@TheGlobalCitizen/social-media-a-triumph-or-tragedy-d302d646824e.

Cameron Jenkins, "How Social Media Made Me a Global Citizen," Newhouse, February 7, 2017. http://newhousesocialmedia.syr.edu/how-social-media-made-me-a-global-citizen.

Daniel McLaughlin, "Mass Migration Guided by Mobiles and Social Media," *Irish Times*, September 9, 2015. https://www.irishtimes.com/news/world/europe/mass-migration-guided-by-mobiles-and-social-media-1.2344662.

Amy Mitchell, Heather Brown, and Emily Guskin, "The Role of Social Media in the Arab Uprisings," Pew Research Center, November 28, 2012. http://www.journalism.org/2012/11/28/role-social-media-arab-uprisings.

Manisha Pathak-Shelat, "Social Media and Youth: Implications for Global Ditizenship Education," Springer, January 12, 2018. https://link.springer.com/chapter/10.1057/978-1-137-59733-5_34.

Emma Somers, "News vs. Newsfeed: The Impact of Social Media on Global Citizenship Education," *Policy & Practice*, Spring 2017. https://www.developmenteducationreview.com/issue/issue-24/news-versus-newsfeed-impact-social-media-global-citizenship-education.

GLOBAL VIEWPOINTS

CHAPTER 4

Citizenship of the Future

Viewpoint 1

Citizenship Can and Should Be Taught

UNESCO

In the following viewpoint, the United Nations Educational, Scientific and Cultural Organization (UNESCO) argues that positive citizenship must be achieved through education and that knowledge of human rights is paramount. The authors maintain that people must learn and embrace the fact that they are entitled to all the civil and political rights as afforded by the country in which they live and that every nation should strive to provide such rights to their citizens. UNESCO seeks to create peaceful solutions to global issues through education, science, and cultural cooperation.

As you read, consider the following questions:

1. How does UNESCO define citizenship education?
2. Have you experienced what you can describe as citizenship education in your school? If so, how have you implemented it?
3. According to the viewpoint, can citizenship education be taught in an unbiased manner, or do disagreements over the definition of citizenship preclude that possibility?

Citizenship education can be defined as educating children, from early childhood, to become clear-thinking and

"Citizenship Education for the 21st Century," UNESCO. http://www.unesco.org/education/tlsf/mods/theme_b/interact/mod07task03/appendix.htm.

enlightened citizens who participate in decisions concerning society. "Society" is here understood in the special sense of a nation with a circumscribed territory which is recognized as a state.

A knowledge of the nation's institutions, and also an awareness that the rule of law applies to social and human relationships, obviously form part of any citizenship education course. Taken in this sense, citizenship education is based on the distinction between:

- the individual as a subject of ethics and law, entitled to all the rights inherent in the human condition (human rights); and
- the citizen—entitled to the civil and political rights recognized by the national constitution of the country concerned.

All human beings are both individuals and citizens of the society to which they belong. Therefore, human rights and citizen rights are interdependent.

Men, women and children all come into the world as individual human beings. Thanks to the immense historical conquest of human rights, we are equal, in rights and dignity, to all other human beings. When citizenship education has the purpose of "educating future citizens" it must necessarily address children, young people and adults, who are living beings, having the status of human beings endowed with conscience and reason. It cannot, therefore, exclude consideration of individuals as subjects, each with individual characteristics.

Moreover, human rights include civil and political rights, the latter obviously relating to the rights and obligations of citizens. Thus a comprehensive human rights education takes account of citizenship, and considers that good citizenship is connected with human rights as a whole.

Conversely, citizenship education which trains "good" citizens, ie. citizens aware of the human and political issues at stake in their society or nation, requires from each citizen ethical and moral qualities. All forms of citizenship education inculcate (or aim at inculcating) respect for others and recognition of the equality of all human beings; and at combating all forms of discrimination (racist, gender-based, religious, etc.) by fostering a spirit of tolerance and peace among human beings.

Thus, when we speak of the purposes to be ascribed to either citizenship education (producing citizens with moral qualities) or human rights education (comprising a knowledge of the social and political rights of all human beings, and their recognition) we inevitably end up with the complementarity between citizenship and human rights.

Depending on the cultural traditions of each education system, we shall have, in some cases, civics education, comprising a knowledge of human rights and their exercise, and in others, human rights education, stressing civil and political rights as the basis of citizenship, and hence the national features assumed by these rights and guaranteed by states.

Bearing in mind this complementarity, citizenship education means not only "educating citizens" but also "training children for adulthood and citizenship."

Citizenship education has, therefore, three main objectives:

- educating people in citizenship and human rights through an understanding of the principles and institutions [which govern a state or nation];
- learning to exercise one's judgement and critical faculty; and
- acquiring a sense of individual and community responsibilities.

These three objectives correspond both to educating the individual as a subject of ethics and law, and to educating citizens. These objectives suggest four major themes for citizenship education:

- The relations between individuals and society: individual and collective freedoms, and rejection of any kind of discrimination.
- The relations between citizens and the government: what is involved in democracy and the organization of the state.
- The relations between the citizen and democratic life.

- The responsibility of the individual and the citizen in the international community.

Democratic Culture and Citizenship Education

If there is one idea inherent in civics education, because it concerns politics and institutions, it is the idea of democracy.

Comprehensive citizenship education cannot dispense with this concept or with a knowledge of the institutions that enable a country to function democratically.

Rather than confining ourselves to noting and describing institutions (the necessary but not sufficient requirement for civics education), we should explain how the operation of the machinery of state respects government of the people by the people, and makes it accountable to citizens.

However, this way of tackling democracy may seem remote and foreign to the world of school and of children. It is therefore desirable to imbue the whole of school life with a culture of democracy.

Educational practice is of equal value with knowledge when we come to tackle civics education. One of the major flaws in civics instruction has been that it fails to bring democracy to life in schools, and remains at the stage of merely enunciating principles and describing institutions. When the organization of a school does not lead to a democratic mode of operating on which pupils can give their opinions, children and adolescents lose interest in citizenship and see only the mismatch between what adults say and what they do, between knowledge and action, a mismatch which they usually call "hypocrisy."

Schools should therefore set up "governing boards" with representatives of pupils and staff, and other bodies in which pupils express their views and in which decisions are taken in consultation with everyone, both young people and adults. The representation of pupils in these various bodies can and should be achieved by an open election system which has the same qualities of transparency as in any democracy worthy of the name.

If we are to develop a credible civics education, respect for others—pupils and teachers, administrators and minor employees—and non-violence in attitudes and behaviour must be the rule in schools.

Respect for others, and their dignity, in the same way as the self-respect of a free autonomous individual, springs from each individual's personal ethic, the will to "live together, with and for others in just institutions."

These qualities, whether described as "moral" or "ethical," are required of all human beings and all citizens. They form part of both civic "virtues" and individual "virtues." They enable each individual to live as a "good" citizen.

In other words, in citizenship education, respect for the "Other," regarded as one's equal, with his or her individual differences and distinctive physical, intellectual and cultural features, is to be explained and above all experienced in daily life in all schools. Based on these principles of equal dignity and respect for others, citizenship education has the task of combating all forms of negative discrimination and racism, sexism and religious fanaticism.

Thus citizenship education can be regarded as an ethical (or moral) education as well as education in citizenship.

A New Way of Teaching Citizenship Education

The introduction and continuance in schools of a democratic culture forbid dogmatism in any kind of civics education. The methods and approaches chosen are those based on discussion among pupils and between pupils and teachers, and make provision for children and young people to speak and express themselves. Modes of expression may be varied: in addition to oral exchanges, drawings, songs, poems, different kinds of written material are excellent instruments for reflection on citizenship, democracy, justice, freedom and peace.

In a democracy, citizenship education seeks to educate citizens who will be free to make their own judgements and hold their own convictions. Compliance with existing laws should not prevent citizens from seeking and planning better and ever more just laws. Respect for law, which is one of the objectives of civics education, calls not for blind submission to rules and laws already passed but the ability to participate in drawing them up.

One of the practical tasks of citizenship education is therefore to look at the rules governing a school, improve them and reformulate them.

The values transmitted by citizenship education are not dogmatic principles laid down once and for all. A living culture calls for the creation of new values, although they should all be judged by the criterion of respect for others and for human dignity.

Thus, with regard to the laws and values accepted by an entire social group, citizenship education can in no way be a catalogue of set questions and answers. Citizenship education should be the forum which gives rise to and nurtures a genuine culture of discussion. Whatever the problem posed, such as the ongoing development of humanity or the stability of the rule of law, an exchange of ideas, notions, judgements and individual opinions is necessary. Even among young children, dialogue of this kind is possible.

Citizenship education needs also to be taught in ways that bring out the ever-constant link between knowledge and practice. The interaction between concepts and action gradually produces the ability to think in terms of values and to refer to them. Values are universal when they concern human rights: for example, the values of liberty, dignity, solidarity and tolerance. As they are firmly anchored and promoted in different cultures they can also concern a region of the world or even a special country, nation or religion. All should be made the subject of discussion and reflection and be studied in each course of citizenship education.

In other words, citizenship education is based on knowledge, practice and values that constantly interact. To be precise, let us say that awareness of the necessary reference to values gradually gives rise to practices and action which are themselves related to knowledge and skills about human rights and the institutions that regulate life in society. Pupils benefiting in this way from citizenship education learn step by step that citizenship unfolds and develops in a society imbued with values and in the human community as a whole.

Global Dimensions in Citizenship Education

The large worldwide population flows that are a characteristic feature of the modern world mean that schools cater for children from different cultural backgrounds. This cultural heterogeneity should be regarded as an opportunity for citizenship education.

In this situation, children are all required to mingle with and thus learn about and understand cultures other than their own. Far from blurring the cultural diversity of pupils, citizenship education can bring out the value of differences while respecting and affirming the universality of human rights principles. Respect for others—a universal principle—means, in the daily life of the school, a dialogue with others, and taking an interest in other family lifestyles, social habits and cultural practices. Citizenship education is the ideal forum, since discussion on social issues can be organized so that opinions can be expressed on ways of looking at the world, in other words, on cultures.

This is a new form of action to combat racism. Racism is frequently due to the ignorance in which children are reared in respect of cultures other than that which is the majority culture of their country. Through a knowledge of these other cultures and the very existence of multicultural life in the classroom, children are fortified against despising the "Other" and against hostile indifference, both of which are sources of racist behaviour.

Conclusion

The problem posed by citizenship education is how to blend together the particular and the universal, the national and the international, the individual and society. The difficulty can be solved by integrating human rights education in this new subject, civics education.

This approach opens up new paths for education for peace, human rights and democracy.

Thus, citizenship education addresses both the individual and the citizen and provides an avenue for each individual citizen to acquire an understanding of the issues of peace in the world, and the challenges of the globalisation of economic, environmental and cultural problems.

Since sustainable development of human beings and the world they live in is linked to the quality of education, the time has come to regard citizenship education as a vital part of any education system and any teaching programme.

Viewpoint 2

In the United States, "Impact Volunteering" Can Lay a Foundation for Civic Renewal

Myung J. Lee and Peter Levine

In the following viewpoint, Myung J. Lee and Peter Levine argue the importance of citizen engagement and creating initiatives to strengthen society and empower people. The authors believe that the more citizens who work at the community level, the stronger the entire society will become. They cite efforts in American communities that have brought positive results in the knowledge that volunteering is a necessary component. Lee is the executive director of Cities of Service. Levine is the Lincoln Filene Professor of Citizenship and Public Affairs in the Jonathan M. Tisch College of Civic Life at Tufts University.

As you read, consider the following questions:

1. What is the new model for citizen engagement as laid out in the viewpoint?
2. How do the authors cite an effort in Birmingham, Alabama, as an example of successful volunteerism?
3. Why do the authors bring up the name of philosopher Hannah Arendt in making their points?

"A New Model for Citizen Engagement," by Myung J. Lee and Peter Levine, Foundation Center, October 26, 2016, Published in Fall 2016 Stanford Social Innovation Review. Reprinted by permission.

In 2013, the city of Birmingham, Alabama, implemented Love Your Block, a nationwide program that awards small grants to local volunteer groups that propose projects designed to improve their neighborhoods. Before issuing a request for proposals, the city conducts extensive outreach to those groups to hear their concerns and to discuss potential solutions on which they and various city agencies can collaborate. The groups then develop and submit proposals, and the city makes a series of grants, which range in size from $500 to $2,000. Staff members from city agencies also work with the neighborhood groups to help them implement their projects. Throughout this process, citizen volunteers engage directly with local officials in setting priorities for civic improvement. And they achieve concrete results: As of January 2015, Love Your Block volunteers in sixteen Birmingham neighborhoods had removed more than 26,000 square feet of graffiti, disposed of more than 167,000 pounds of trash and debris, planted more than 500 trees, and revitalized 117 blocks.

As impressive as those outputs are, Love Your Block has also generated broad social outcomes. A statistician in the Birmingham Police Department reviewed crime data in the sixteen target neighborhoods at the beginning of the first year of the program and again at the end of that year. In those neighborhoods, overall crime—a category that includes violent crime—fell by 11 percent during the first year of the initiative. What's more, those neighborhoods collectively experienced a 13 percent reduction in property theft and a 16 percent reduction in auto theft. Although other factors certainly contributed to these results, there are reasons to believe that the social cohesion fostered by Love Your Block has played a notable part in reducing crime in the targeted neighborhoods. Testing is now under way in thirteen other cities to gauge the impact that programs like Love Your Block have on public safety.

Love Your Block is an initiative of Cities of Service, a nonprofit organization that works to promote results-driven citizen engagement. Founded in 2009 by Michael Bloomberg, then-mayor of New York City, Cities of Service has built a coalition that includes more than two hundred cities in the United States and the United Kingdom. One of us (Myung J. Lee) serves as executive director of the organization.

Strong evidence has accumulated to show that communities are more likely to succeed when citizens engage with each other—and with public sector leaders—in certain ways. At the crux of our model of citizen engagement are three elements. First, people in a community should deliberate on public issues. Second, they should collaborate on solving local problems. And third, they should connect with others to form long-term civic relationships.

That kind of citizen engagement is not particularly robust or widespread in the United States today. Between the 1970s and the 1990s, the proportion of Americans who said that they had attended a community meeting declined from more than 60 percent to slightly more than 30 percent. Over the same period, the percentage of Americans who said that they had worked to address a community problem fell by almost twenty points. The proportion of people who follow local news has also been declining steadily since the 1970s.[1] The larger consequences of this trend are readily apparent: Institutions like the US Congress have become highly polarized and dysfunctional. And the 2016 presidential election is on its way to being the least civil national election in modern history.

US communities, however, have an often-overlooked asset for promoting citizen engagement: city-sponsored volunteer service programs. Volunteering on its own does not necessarily produce better outcomes for a community. But municipal service programs, we believe, hold the promise of enabling Americans to achieve a deeper and more consequential form of engagement than most of them now have with their communities. By transforming traditional volunteering into what we call "impact volunteering," civic leaders and citizens can lay the groundwork for improving community-level outcomes. In an impact volunteering effort such as Love Your Block, participants go beyond simply contributing hours of service to local projects. They also pursue the vital work of deliberation, collaboration, and connection.

Communities suffer when wide gaps exist between government and civil society—and between government officials and citizens. By engaging volunteers as partners in defining and solving local problems, community leaders can narrow those gaps and thereby advance the cause of civic renewal.

Why Citizen Engagement Matters

According to the philosopher Hannah Arendt, the founders of the American republic derived certain lessons from their experience of public service: They learned "that no one could be called happy without his share in public happiness, that no one could be called free without his experience in public freedom"—which, for Arendt, meant active participation in public affairs—"and that no one could be called either happy or free without participating, and having a share, in public power."[2] They learned, in other words, that citizen engagement is an intrinsically valuable aspect of human life. By working with their fellow citizens on matters of public concern, people experience a special kind of satisfaction.

But the benefits of citizen engagement extend beyond the rewards that individuals gain from civic work. When people work closely with one another and with local institutions—with city agencies, nonprofit organizations, and the like—they build strong and healthy communities. And as a result, those communities achieve impressive outcomes in areas ranging from education to environmental protection. In recent years, scholars have produced a wide range of studies that illustrate this effect, and in those studies they use terms such as "social capital" and "social cohesion" to describe the kind of value that citizen engagement creates.

Consider the issue of public safety. The sociologist Robert J. Sampson, in a landmark investigation of Chicago, explored the role that various factors play in a city. One such factor is "collective efficacy," as Sampson calls it.[3] He assembled a wide array of data to measure that quality—from the number of neighborhood watch groups in a community to the likelihood that residents who found a stamped, addressed envelope on the street would take time to put the envelope in a mailbox. For one study, Sampson and other researchers used a ten-item survey to measure the collective efficacy of various neighborhoods. They asked residents of those communities, for example, whether "people around here are willing to help their neighbors" and whether "people in this neighborhood can be trusted." As it turned out, neighborhoods in which respondents scored high on that survey exhibited relatively low levels of violent crime. That result held even when the researchers took into account factors such as income and race.[4]

Or take the issue of education. Robert D. Putnam, a professor of public policy at Harvard University, has created an index of "social capital" that tracks participation in civic affairs and volunteering, among other measures. In one study, he examined test scores and graduation rates in all fifty US states and found that social capital was a stronger predictor of student success than spending on schools, the demographic composition of schools, class size, or teachers' salaries.[5]

Social capital also appears to enable greater economic mobility. A team led by Raj Chetty, a professor of economics at Stanford University, has demonstrated that where people in the United States grow up has a significant effect on whether they are able to move up the economic ladder. The team has identified five attributes of communities that have high levels of economic mobility, and social capital is one of them.[6]

One of us (Peter Levine) joined with Kei Kawashima-Ginsberg and Chaeyoon Lim to investigate the connection between social cohesion and economic performance. Looking specifically at the aftermath of the 2008–09 recession, the team found a wide divergence in how well cities and states recovered from that event. Among states that have similar economic circumstances, for example, those with high levels of social cohesion regained jobs that had been lost during the recession at a 20 percent higher rate than those with low levels of social cohesion.[7] (To measure social cohesion, the researchers developed a composite of variables that range from how often people socialize with friends and family members to the number of nonprofit organizations per capita.)

Other research suggests that civic engagement helps to improve environmental outcomes. Kent Portney, a professor at the Bush School of Government and Public Service at Texas A&M University, has shown that cities with well-regarded sustainability policies almost always rely on intensive engagement processes to develop those policies.[8]

How exactly does citizen engagement lead to positive social outcomes? Research exists to support several explanations.

- Engaged citizens gain skills and contacts that help them succeed in other aspects of their lives. Studies of labor markets in Germany, the United Kingdom, and the United States demonstrate that "people skills"—as measured by, for example, a preference for working in collaboration with others—have substantial and growing market value.[9]
- Engaged citizens develop norms of trust and collaboration that enable them to contribute to their local economy. Francis Fukuyama, a scholar based at Stanford University, notes that numerous studies from around the world show a correlation between higher levels of social trust and higher rates of entrepreneurial activity.[10]
- Engaged citizens push to achieve effective legislation and effective performance from government. Putnam, in a classic study, found that devolving power from a national to a regional level in Italy worked well in regions that had high levels of civic participation, in part because people in those regions demanded clean and responsive government, but it failed in regions where participation was low.[11]

What Citizen Engagement Requires

To reap the full benefits of involving people in civic life, people and their leaders must pursue all three aspects of citizen engagement: communicating about issues of shared concern (deliberation), working together to address those issues (collaboration), and forging effective and enduring relationships (connection). In an optimal case, these aspects reinforce one another: People gather in groups to decide what to do. Then they work in concert to implement that decision. And then, as a result of these efforts, they form tight networks that support continued engagement.

Deliberation

The American system of government was built on the assumption that citizens would deliberate with each other. In his draft of the First Amendment to the US Constitution, James Madison included this explanation of its purpose: "The people shall not be restrained from peaceably assembling and consulting for their common good."[12] The final version of the amendment omitted that line, but clearly Madison believed that "consulting for [the] common good" was an essential element of the US constitutional system. Woodrow Wilson made a similar point in a speech that he gave while running for president in 1912: "The whole purpose of democracy is that we may hold counsel with one another."[13]

When citizens talk and listen to people who are different from them, they enlarge their understanding of public issues. They learn to check their own values and assumptions against those of other people, and they make themselves accountable to their fellow citizens. Along the way, they build the kind of consensus that makes political action possible.

Collaboration

Deliberation is not enough, however. Citizens must be able to follow their talk with collective action. They must be able to work together—across different sectors, across the boundaries that separate citizens from civic leaders—on efforts to create better outcomes for their communities. Citizens, in other words, need to cooperate to achieve the goals that emerge through deliberation. To be effective, collaboration must also include an element of reflection: Citizens should discuss and evaluate what they have done and then hold themselves accountable for the results.

A study by the sociologist Sean Safford highlights the necessity of collaboration. Safford compared the trajectories of Allentown, Pennsylvania, and Youngstown, Ohio. The collapse of the US steel industry devastated both cities, but Allentown rebounded and Youngstown did not. Allentown, Safford discovered, had a diverse network of overlapping associations—including both municipal and private sector entities—that could develop a coordinated response to the city's social and economic challenges. Youngstown also had a large number of local associations, but the membership of those groups tended not to overlap, and their members did not work together effectively.[14]

Connection

Democracy depends on civic relationships—on voluntary ties among peers who share an interest in improving their community. Civic relationships require certain essential attributes, including loyalty, trust, and hope. In the United States, these attributes have become less and less prevalent. According to survey research, for instance, the proportion of Americans who say that they trust other people has dropped over the past four decades. And that shift is generational: Each new cohort exhibits a lower degree of social trust than the preceding cohort.[15] But it is not too late to reverse that trend. By connecting with their fellow citizens, Americans can rebuild the sense of trust that helps create strong communities.

When Volunteering Has Impact

In cities and towns across the United States, municipal volunteer programs attract large numbers of citizens who commit time, passion, skill, and energy to community activities. In 2015, according to the Corporation for National and Community

Service, 62.8 million Americans volunteered 7.9 billion hours of service.[16] And according to data gathered by the US Census Bureau, 35 percent of Americans participate in at least one voluntary association.[17] In our view, the vast scale of volunteering offers an important opportunity to increase the scope and impact of citizen engagement.

Volunteering per se is not a predictor of better social outcomes. Although volunteers benefit the people whom they directly serve, their efforts do not automatically produce positive results at a community level. Kawashima-Ginsberg, Lim, and Levine tested the relationship between the rates of volunteering in counties, cities, and states and the economic outcomes of the same communities, and they found no link between these variables.[18] But such findings mainly reflect the limitations of traditional volunteer programs. In that kind of program, people give hours of service to community projects, but neither they nor local leaders work to connect that service to a larger strategy of citizen engagement.

Impact volunteering, by contrast, adjusts such shortcomings by involving community members in deliberation, collaboration, and connection. By treating citizens as partners, leaders can transform their volunteer programs into participatory processes in which citizens and public officials develop a shared vision, set long-term and short-term goals for their community, and then work together to pursue those goals. Ultimately, impact volunteering is not only about pursuing discrete projects but also about creating social capital and increasing social cohesion.

By way of example, consider Path Finders, an impact volunteering initiative operated by the city of Orlando, Florida. (Orlando is a member of the Cities of Service coalition.) Path Finders is a six-week-long afterschool program that aims to help middle-school students increase their career potential. Volunteers from various industries and professions work to help students develop an individualized path toward a successful future. Students in the program investigate career alternatives, explore their own career goals, and then create an academic plan that supports those goals. Results from the program illustrate the value of engaging volunteers in this way: During the yearlong evaluation period that followed one iteration of the program, every participating student achieved a grade point average of 2.5 or higher, and no student underwent suspension or expulsion proceedings. In a survey of Path Finders students, 74 percent of them reported that they saw a connection between their education and their career path, and 88 percent of them reported that their desire to graduate from high school had increased. Path Finders, in sum, demonstrates how a city government can raise social capital by building relationships among citizens.

How Impact Volunteering Can Thrive

Two ingredients that help turn a conventional volunteering program into an impact volunteering program are the use of metrics and the active involvement of municipal government. (Cities of Service, for example, urges participating cities to establish and collect outcomes metrics, and it calls on city agencies to act as full-fledged partners of their citizen volunteers.)

Using Metrics

Officials who administer volunteer programs and citizens who serve in those programs should select measurable outcomes and track their progress toward meeting such outcomes. This focus on metrics shifts the framework of volunteering from one in which volunteers garner praise simply because they do unpaid work ("it's nice") to one in which they work to achieve measurable results ("it's necessary"). A commitment to tracking outcomes also promotes transparency and a sense of shared purpose, and those benefits in turn help deepen relationships among volunteers and between volunteers and city officials.

In Austin, Texas, for instance, city staff members trained volunteers to identify and report the occurrence of invasive plant species in the city's parkland. The work of these volunteers helped the city assess the extent of this problem, and it provided staff members with specific data that they could use to make a funding request—which ultimately was successful—to the Austin City Council. Later, the city was able to dedicate a staff member to working with volunteers to remove the invasive species from parks throughout Austin.

All the same, the use of metrics is no substitute for citizen engagement. Melody Barnes and Paul Schmitz, in a recent article in *Stanford Social Innovation Review*, acknowledge that there is "an economic and a moral imperative for adopting data-driven approaches" to social policy. "Given persistently limited budgets, public and nonprofit leaders must direct funds to programs and initiatives that use data to show that they are achieving impact," they write. Yet they also emphasize the need for continued public engagement in that process: "Data-driven solutions will be feasible and sustainable only if leaders create and implement those solutions with the active participation of people in the communities that they target."[19]

Enlisting Municipal Government

Citizens do not need to work with local government in order to pursue deliberation, collaboration, and connection. Still, municipalities can and should play a leading role in citizen engagement. They have resources—expertise, access to data, legal authority, funding—that they can share with local groups. In addition, they have power to convene cross-sector gatherings where citizens can address matters of common concern. Communities need both robust horizontal relationships among their own organizations and tight connections to city hall. Sampson, in his study of Chicago, found that neighborhoods flourish when local leaders can form networks that connect them not only with each other but also with public sector institutions. And indeed, one advantage of the impact volunteering model is that it changes how citizens and city governments relate to each other.

That model, for example, can strengthen relationships between city agencies and historically underserved groups. In Austin, an

AmeriCorps VISTA participant who was serving at city hall used the Love Your Block program to engage low-income communities that typically find it hard to access municipal resources. To help people in those communities apply for Love Your Block mini-grants, she hired a contractor to translate application documents into Spanish, and she facilitated two grant-writing workshops. Of the thirty-eight applications that Austin received for these grants, thirty-five came from neighborhoods where the average income was below that of the city as a whole.

Impact volunteering practices also enhance the ability of citizens to deal with local problems. Instead of merely lodging a complaint at city hall, they can engage in two-way communication with government officials. In Seattle, as part of a program called Find It, Fix It, the city's mayor walks through neighborhoods alongside residents to identify and discuss local challenges. The heads of city departments and other city employees join the mayor on these walks, and these officials then work with citizens to address the problems that they spot along the way. Most important, the officials report back to neighborhood residents about whether and how they are able to solve each problem.

Another important feature of the impact volunteering model is that it breaks down the artificial distinction between citizens and city employees. That distinction is harmful because it obscures the fact that civil servants are also citizens. People who work for city government often have a particularly keen sense of civic welfare. Consider Tanya Meeks, who has served for many years as community affairs officer in the police department of Flint, Michigan. A few years ago, after budget cuts resulted in a layoff of more than one-third of the city's police force, Meeks lost her position. But she continued to work on community safety issues as a civilian. "I came back to the city to work on neighborhoods … not in uniform, no cruiser," she says. "It was not about me; it was about services … The work never stopped. We kept rolling." Later, she was able to return to the force, and she served as coordinator for a volunteer program that Flint launched with support from Cities of Service.

The Question of Civic Renewal

To meet the challenges that Americans currently face, communities in the United States need to increase the scale and the quality of citizen engagement. They need, in short, to begin an effort of civic renewal. So how can leaders and citizens begin that effort? People in various sectors have developed approaches to answering this question. But impact volunteering, we argue, offers an especially compelling answer. By enabling volunteers to deliberate, collaborate, and connect—by enabling them not only to contribute hours of service but also to take part in planning and initiating civic improvements—communities can transform those volunteers into engaged citizens.

Americans respond well to direct calls to participate in civic activities. But relatively few of them have the ability on their own to transform traditional volunteering into impact volunteering. Civic leaders who oversee municipal service programs do have the resources—the skills, the experience, the convening power—that are necessary to achieve civic renewal in their jurisdictions. What's more, they have an incentive to do so: Their communities prosper when levels of social cohesion are high. They, along with their volunteer partners, can be a nucleus of an effort to renew citizen engagement.

Notes

1. Peter Levine, *We Are the Ones We Have Been Waiting For: The Promise of Civic Renewal in America*, New York: Oxford University Press, 2013, pp. 94–96.
2. Hannah Arendt, *On Revolution*, New York: Penguin Classics, 2006, p. 247.
3. Robert J. Sampson, *Great American City: Chicago and the Enduring Neighborhood Effect*, Chicago: University of Chicago Press, 2012.
4. Robert J. Sampson, Stephen W. Raudenbush, and Felton Earls, "Neighborhoods and Violent Crime: A Multilevel Study of Collective Efficacy," *Science*, 277, 1997, pp. 918–924.
5. Robert D. Putnam, "Community-Based Social Capital and Educational Performance," in Diane Ravitch and Joseph P. Viteritti, eds., *Making Good Citizens: Education and Civil Society*, New Haven, Conn.: Yale University Press, 2001, pp. 58–95.

6. Raj Chetty, Nathaniel Hendren, Patrick Kline, and Emmanuel Saez, "Where Is the Land of Opportunity? The Geography of Intergenerational Mobility in the United States," *Quarterly Journal of Economics*, 129, 2014, pp. 1553–1623.
7. Kei Kawashima-Ginsberg, Chaeyoon Lim, and Peter Levine, "Civic Health and Unemployment II: The Case Builds," National Conference on Citizenship, 2012.
8. Kent Portney, "Civic Engagement and Sustainable Cities in the United States," *Public Administration Review*, 65, 2005, pp. 579–591.
9. Lex Borghans, Bas ter Weel, and Bruce A. Weinberg, "People People: Social Capital and the Labor-Market Outcomes of Underrepresented Groups," National Bureau of Economic Research Working Paper No. 11985, 2006.
10. Francis Fukuyama, *Trust: The Social Virtues and the Creation of Prosperity*, New York: Free Press, 1995.
11. Robert D. Putnam, *Making Democracy Work: Civic Traditions in Modern Italy*, Princeton, N.J.: Princeton University Press, 1993. See also Jeffrey M. Berry, Kent E. Portney, and Kenneth Thomson, *The Rebirth of Urban Democracy*, Washington, D.C.: Brookings Institution, 1993; Kent E. Portney and Jeffrey M. Berry, "Participation and the Pursuit of Sustainability in U.S. Cities," *Urban Affairs Review*, 46, 2010, pp. 119–139.
12. Ralph Ketcham, *Framed for Posterity: The Enduring Philosophy of the Constitution*, Lawrence, Kan.: University Press of Kansas, 1993, p. 100.
13. Woodrow Wilson, *The New Freedom: A Call for the Emancipation of the Generous Energies of a People*, New York: Doubleday, Page & Company, 1913.
14. Sean Safford, *Why the Garden Club Couldn't Save Youngstown: The Transformation of the Rust Belt*, Cambridge, Mass.: Harvard University Press, 2009.
15. Jean M. Twenge, W. Keith Campbell, and Nathan T. Carter, "Declines in Trust in Others and Confidence in Institutions Among American Adults and Late Adolescents, 1972–2012," *Psychological Science*, 25, 2014, pp. 1914–1923.
16. Corporation for National and Community Service (CNCS), "Volunteering and Civic Life in America 2015."
17. Corporation for National and Community Service (CNCS) and National Conference on Citizenship, "Civic Life in America: Key Findings on the Civic Health of the Nation," September 2010.
18. Kawashima-Ginsberg, Lim, and Levine, "Civic Health and Unemployment II."
19. Melody Barnes and Paul Schmitz, "Community Engagement Matters (Now More Than Ever)," *Stanford Social Innovation Review*, Spring 2016.

Viewpoint 3

We Should Aim for a Practical Citizenship

Michael Schudson

In the following excerpted viewpoint, Michael Schudson laments the lack of civic engagement as proved by poor voter participation and involvement in the election process. It is interesting to note that this viewpoint was written in 1994. Although future events such as the 2018 midterm elections proved that voters will show up to the polls if greatly motivated by candidates and events, the author's concerns of nearly thirty years ago still resonate. Schudson offers personal experiences and historical context as he cites the founding of the United States and says that citizens must take greater responsibility to forge their own future and that of the nation in which they live. Schudson is an author and professor of journalism at Columbia University.

As you read, consider the following questions:

1. Do the points made by the author in 1994 still have validity today despite the changing times and events?
2. How have events since the 2016 American presidential election changed views about political participation?
3. How do the personal experiences of the author as he relates them in this piece further his arguments?

If recent trends hold up, only about one of every three eligible voters will show up at the polls this fall. Inevitably, many will conclude that Americans have once again failed as citizens. The problem, however, may not be individual failure so much as our contemporary conception of how democratic citizenship ought to work. Nothing puts that conception into clearer perspective than changes in the act of voting over the past 200 years.

Imagine yourself a voter in the world of colonial Virginia where George Washington, Patrick Henry, and Thomas Jefferson learned their politics. As a matter of law, you must be a white male owning at least a modest amount of property. Your journey to vote may take several hours since there is probably only one polling place in the county. As you approach the courthouse, you see the sheriff supervising the election. Two candidates for office stand before you, both of them members of prominent local families. You watch the most prominent members of the community, the leading landowner and clergyman, cast their votes, and you know whom they have supported because they announce their votes in loud, clear voices. You do the same and then step over to the candidate for whom you have voted, and he treats you to a glass of rum punch. Your vote has been an act of restating and reaffirming the social hierarchy of a community where no one but a local notable would think of standing for office.

Now imagine you are in eighteenth century Massachusetts rather than Virginia. The model of voting is different, as you elect town selectmen and representatives at a town meeting. But, like Virginia, the New England model reflects an organic view that the polity has a single common good and that the leaders of locally prominent, wealthy, and well established families can be trusted to represent it. Dissent and conflict are no more acceptable in New England than in Virginia.

Move the clock ahead to the nineteenth century, as mass political parties cultivate a new democratic order. Now there is much more bustle around the polling place. The area is crowded with the banners and torches of rival parties. Election day is not set off from other days but is the culmination of a campaign of several months. You must still be a white male but not necessarily of property. During the campaign, you have marched in torchlight processions in military uniform with a club of like-minded men from your party. They may accompany you to the polls. If you were not active in the campaign, you may be roused on election day by a party worker to escort you on foot or by carriage. On the road, you may encounter clubs or groups from rival parties, and it would not be unusual if fisticuffs or even guns were to dissuade you from casting a ballot after all.

If you do proceed to the ballot box, you may step more lively with the encouragement of a dollar or two from the party—less a bribe than an acknowledgment that voting is a service to your party. A party worker hands you a colored ballot with the printed names of the party's candidates. You may also receive a slightly smaller ballot with the same names on it that can be surreptitiously placed inside the other so that you can cast two ballots rather than one. You are willing to do so not out of a strong sense that your party offers better public policies but because your party is your party, just as, in our own day, your high school is your high school. In any event, parties tend to be more devoted to distributing offices than to advocating policies.

Now turn to the early twentieth century as Progressive era reforms cleanse voting of what made it both compelling and, by our standards, corrupt. Reformers find the emphasis in campaigns on spectacle rather than substance much too emotional. They pioneer what they term an "educational campaign" that stresses the distribution of pamphlets on the issues rather than parades of solidarity. They pass legislation to ensure a secret ballot. They enact voter registration statutes. They help create an atmosphere in which it becomes more common for traditionally loyal party newspapers to "bolt" from party-endorsed candidates. They insist on official state ballots rather than party ballots and in some states develop state-approved voter information booklets rather than leaving education up to the parties themselves. At the same time, civil service reform limits the rewards parties can distribute to loyal partisans.

The world we experience today at the polls has been handed down to us from these reforms. What does voting look like and feel like today?

I asked my students at the University of California, San Diego to write about their experience of voting in 1992. Many of them had never voted before; hardly any had voted in a presidential election. It is something they looked forward to doing, especially those who supported Clinton. Still, some students felt a let-down in the act of voting:

> As I punched in the holes on my voting card, a slight sense of disappointment clouded my otherwise cheerful mood. First of all, the building behind Revelle Bargain Books was not what I had always imagined as a polling place. How could a location this close to the all-you-can-eat cafeteria be the site of a vote to choose the leader of our nation? Second, I could not understand why there were no curtains around my booth. As a child I can always remember crawling under curtains in voting booths to spy on my parents. Why couldn't I have those curtains to hide all of my important, private decisions?

Or listen to this student, a Filipino-American who voted for Bush:

> The more I tried to be aware of the political goings-on, through television mainly, the more I became aggravated with the whole situation. Perot represented the evil of a one-man monopoly, while Clinton was a man who knew how to manipulate an audience and use the media. In addition, Hillary reminded me of the stories and comments my parents made about Imelda Marcos. Taxes came to mind every time I considered Bush, but I decided he might be the best qualified candidate.
>
> My Dad was an influential part of my decision to go; not because he urged me to do so, but so that after the election I would finally be able to tell him that I voted.

> Needless to say, no one at the polling site seemed to talk politics, at least not when I was there. The silence did not bother me, though, since I am definitely not confident enough to talk politics to anyone outside of my family!

Or this immigrant Russian:

> My Mom went to vote with me that day (at the polling place in a neighbor's garage). The night before, I had marked my mother's sample ballot with circles around "yes" and "no" on particular propositions and checked the boxes next to "Feinstein" and "Boxer" so she would not forget. The sample ballot is very convenient. The propositions are especially grueling to read. They disguise themselves in legal/state jargon and refuse to give way to meaning.
>
> I felt distantly connected to other voters in other garages who would be making the same vote for change as I would. Nevertheless, I went through my ballot, standing in that cardboard cubicle, in a very ordinary way, feeling that I was, most likely, insignificant and that my views would find no representation. I remember guessing on some local offices, like county supervisor, and trying not to pick a "Christian right" candidate.

The individuality and jealously guarded privacy of voting today contrasts dramatically with the viva voce process of eighteenth century Virginia or the colorful party ticket voting of the nineteenth century. So do the indecision and uncertainty. The students felt inadequate to the election—and why not? The list of propositions and complex voter information pamphlet in California were overwhelming. My voter information pamphlet for the June 1994 primary ran forty-eight pages—and that was just for city and county offices and referenda. For state offices and ballot measures, a separate publication ran sixty-four pages. The obscurity of many candidates and issues encouraged mass pre-election mailings of leaflet slates of candidates produced by profit-making organizations with no connection to political parties. I received, for instance, "Voter Information Guide for Democrats"

Can Mobile Technology Fight Hunger?

Twenty years ago fax machines were almost everywhere, but today most people would be hard-pressed to recite their company's fax number. Soon they'll probably go the way of the telegraph, becoming dusty museum pieces. Communications technology is changing rapidly, and humanitarian organisations are adapting alongside it.

But how can technology be used to fight food insecurity in a region as large and diverse as east Africa?

Karen Peachey, the British Red Cross' east Africa representative, gives a few ideas: "Mobile phones are everywhere in east Africa, even in many remote areas. If mobile companies could improve access further then people's lives can change. A mobile phone gives you access to information—you can find out that your goat is worth more money than the middleman is offering, meaning you have better access to food, medical care, and education."

Mobile money is another technology that can change lives, and it's hugely popular in east Africa. Mobile phones can be linked to a virtual account, and people easily transfer money from their own account to others'. Mobile money can be used like cash and is particularly important in places like Somalia, which has a sophisticated mobile network, allowing

and "Crime Fighters '94" produced by "Democratic Choice '94." The weary voter had to read the fine print to learn that neither slate was endorsed by the Democratic party.

Whatever else we learn from elections, we are tutored in a sense of helplessness and fundamental inadequacy to the task of citizenship. We are told to be informed but discover that the information required to cast an informed vote is beyond our capacities. We are reminded that the United States has the lowest voter turnout of any democracy but rarely told that we have more elections for more levels of government with more elective offices at each level than any other country in the world. We are enjoined by critics of Lockean liberalism to devote ourselves more heartily to the public weal as social beings, but in the primal act of citizenship we face the ballot alone, in privacy, with our own conscience, face to face with our own ignorance.

Somalis to use their mobile phones to send their families money in rural areas.

And Kenyans, as well as using mobile money to send to their families, are using their phones to sms donations to fundraising appeals, like the Kenyans for Kenya appeal which is raising money to help parts of Kenya that are suffering a food crisis.

The Kenya Red Cross has close links with local research institutions, and they work with the Kenya Meteorological Office to understand better where and when the rain will fall—or fail. This means the Red Cross can be prepared and help communities start planning early for a crisis. Getting the information out to vulnerable communities is the next step. What better way to do so than through mobile technology that most people already use, developing partnerships with telecoms companies to make such messages cheap?

Humanitarian organisations need to keep abreast of changes in technology and how communities are using it themselves. We need to be willing to experiment with new ways of using technology—and learn from the experiments that will sometimes fail.

"Mobile Technology Could Be Vital in East Africa's Fight Against Hunger," by Katrina Crew, International Federation of Red Cross and Red Crescent Societies (IFRC), September 16, 2011.

A Burden of Progressivism

We need a new concept of citizenship, one that asks something from us but is not burdened with the impossible expectations of the Progressive model. Contrast what we implicitly expect of ourselves today and what Thomas Jefferson hoped for citizens 200 years ago. In the preamble of Bill 79 to establish universal elementary instruction in Virginia, Jefferson observed that the people normally elect men of standing in the community. The community needs especially to educate these leaders. As for the citizenry at large, Jefferson sought to inculcate through the study of history knowledge that "they may be enabled to know ambition under all its shapes, and prompt to exert their natural powers to defeat its purposes." That was the whole of the citizen's job—watchfulness to defeat ambition.

Citizens were decidedly not to undertake their own evaluation of issues before the legislature. That was the job of representatives. The Founding Fathers assumed that voters would and should choose representatives on the basis of character, not issues. Representatives would have enough in common with the people they represented to keep their "interests" in mind. For the Founding Fathers, elected representatives—not parties, not interest groups, not newspapers, not citizens in the streets—were to make policy.

We have come to ask more of citizens. Today's dominant views about citizenship come from the Progressives' rationalist and ardently individualist worldview. The Progressive impulse was educational—to bring science to politics and professional management to cities, to substitute pamphlets for parades and parlors for streets. The practice of citizenship, at least in campaigning and voting, became privatized, more effortful, more cognitive, and a lot less fun.

In the eighteenth and nineteenth centuries, there was no concern about the people who did not vote. Political science and public discourse began to worry about nonvoters only after World War I when voting rates had declined to a low not reached again until the 1970s. The National Association of Manufacturers, the news media, and other groups responded by designing "get out the vote" campaigns, those largely fruitless moral injunctions to "vote, vote for whomever you choose, but vote." Such slogans were unheard of in the decades of highest voter turnout from 1840 to 1900. You sure as hell did not want people from the other party voting. Campaigns were military efforts. You already knew who stood in your army behind your banner; the task of the campaign was to get them to the polls. Citizenship was social; the Progressives, in the name of rationality and education, changed all that.

The Progressive ideal requires citizens to possess a huge fund of political information and a ceaseless attentiveness to public issues. This could never be. Even at the Constitutional convention of 1787 a delegate observed that people grew "listless" with frequent elections. Fifty years later Tocqueville lamented, "Even when one has won the confidence of a democratic nation, it is a hard matter to attract its attention." A half century thereafter Woodrow Wilson wrote:

> The ordinary citizen cannot be induced to pay much heed to the details unless something else more interesting than the law itself be involved … If the fortunes of a party or the power of a great political leader are staked upon the final vote, he will listen with the keenest interest … but if no such things hang in the balance, he will not turn from his business to listen.

So if, as some people suggest these days, Americans suffer from a political attention deficit disorder, it has been incubating for a long time. Perhaps television or party decline exacerbates it. But public inattention has been a fact of political life, with only momentary escapes, through our history. If this is so, what is a reasonable expectation for citizens, a reasonable standard of citizen competence?

A Practical Citizenship

Under democratic government, as the Founding Fathers constituted it, the representatives of the people could carry on the business of governing without individual citizens becoming experts on the questions of policy placed before the Congress. Similarly, technologies of cognition, as Donald Norman argues in his book *Things That Make Us Smart*, allow us to act more intelligently without being any smarter or performing great feats of memory. We can carry a datebook, consult a dictionary, use a calculator, run spell check. We don't have to keep everything in our heads. Cognition is distributed.

Citizens are not to be created one by one, pouring into each of them enough newspapers, information, or virtuous resolve for them to judge each issue and each candidate rationally. That is where the Progressive vision went wrong. Citizens flourish in an environment that supports worthwhile citizenship activities. We should be intent on creating such an environment, not on turning every voter into an expert.

If, like the Progressives, we take citizenship to be a function of the individual, we are bound to be discouraged. A classical model of citizenship asks that people seek the good of the general, the public. But this is either utopian—people just do not pay that kind of attention—or else undesirable because it honors public life to the exclusion of work-a-day labor or inner spiritual pursuits. A more Lockean, modern, realistic version is that citizens should be moved in public life by self-interest and so should acquire a fair understanding of their own interests and which public policies best serve them. But people's knowledge of public affairs fails even by this standard. Even self-interest in politics is a surprisingly weak reed since the gratifications of private life—getting home on time rather than stopping at the polls to vote, spending seven or eight dollars for a movie rather than for a campaign contribution—are more visible and immediate than the marginal contribution one might make to determining policy by voting, signing a petition, or writing a letter.

How low can we go? We can seek to build a political system where individuals will perform the right actions for their own or the public's interest without knowing much at all. People will do the right thing in general ignorance. User-friendly technology works this way; almost anyone can drive a car while knowing scarcely anything about what makes it run.

In *The Reasoning Voter*, Samuel Popkin suggests we are pretty close to this user-friendly politics already. Relatively little of what voters know, Popkin argues, comes to them as abstract political intelligence. They make intelligent voting decisions based only in small measure on their attending to campaign issues. People have little of the propositional knowledge that models of citizenship demand, but they have more background knowledge than they may realize. They know about economic issues because they have savings accounts, home mortgages, or mutual funds. They have views about health care reform because they know someone personally who has been denied health insurance because of a pre-existing condition. They have enough "by-product information" from daily life to make the broad, either-or choice of a presidential candidate in ways consistent with their own interests and views. Even in presidential primaries, Popkin suggests, shifts in voter allegiance are better explained by a model of "low-information rationality" than by media manipulation or passions run riot.

In elections for school boards and other local contests, however, where public information about candidates is more limited and there are often no party labels (again, thanks to Progressive reforms), voters may find themselves in the polling booth without a clue about whom to support. This is not a new condition, if the humorist Finley Peter Dunne is to be believed: "A rayformer thinks he was ilicted because he was a rayformer, whin th' thruth iv th' matther is he was ilicted because no wan knew him."

[…]

Viewpoint 4

In Africa, Regular Ballots Indicate Progress Towards Ensuring Citizens Are Able to Choose Their Leaders

Carla Kweifio-Okai and Josh Holder

In the following viewpoint, Carla Kweifio-Okai and Josh Holder argue that corruption at government levels has resulted in a lack of democracy in many African nations. This and many other issues have created serious problems for African citizens. The authors, citing the grip of authoritarian leaders who retain power under the guise of free elections throughout that continent, call for changes. They furthermore question the legitimacy of those elections. Kweifio-Okai is a former community coordinator at the Guardian *and works as the communications manager at the International Women's Development Agency. Holder is a visual projects editor at the* Guardian.

As you read, consider the following questions:

1. What has allowed false claims about African democracy to spread?
2. Do the authors provide a sense of optimism or pessimism about the future of African nations and their citizens?
3. How has corruption in government prevented citizens in African countries from improving their lives?

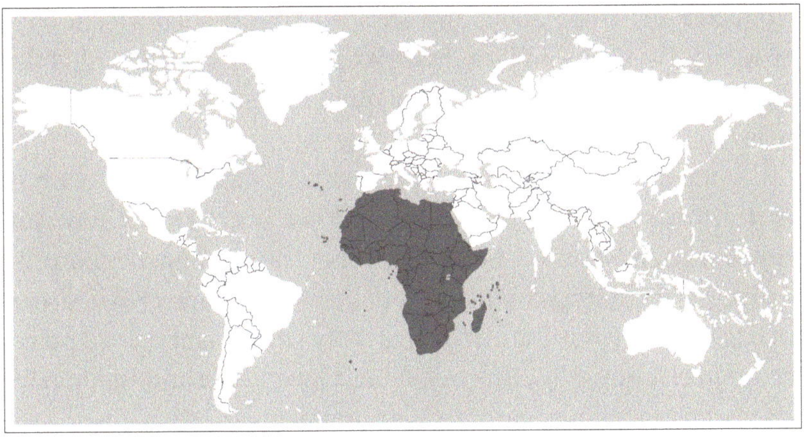

From the US to Uganda, most countries grapple with a democratic deficit. Yet there is a popular perception that Africa lags behind the rest of the world in this most nebulous of political terms. This is despite the fact that millions of people elsewhere in the world live under regimes that can be described as authoritarian, oppressive and undemocratic, while millions of people within Africa enjoy the benefits of relatively good governance.

Former British leader Winston Churchill thought democracy was "the worst form of government, except for all the others." His words lays bare the imperfections of what we call democracy, but also hint at how difficult it is to define.

1. Democracy Is Not Spreading Across Africa

Countries that describe themselves as democratic are members of a very broad church. They range from nations that respect citizens' political freedoms and civil liberties to those that repress dissent and hold elections that are neither free nor fair. Just as other regions of the world display varied systems of governance, there are discrepancies among African countries too.

The Economist Intelligence Unit's democracy index identifies four categories of regime: full democracy, flawed democracy, hybrid and authoritarian. Its 2015 index shows uneven progress in sub-Saharan Africa, but notes a dramatic drop in successful "coups from within" since 2000, and says holding regular elections is now largely commonplace. Even so, the index only awarded full democracy status to Mauritius, a quiet achiever with strong rule of law.

Some countries defy the narrative of a democratic deficit in Africa, however. In its 2016 Freedom in the World report, Freedom House named Nigeria, Liberia and Ivory Coast among the countries with the biggest improvements in political rights and civil liberties. In Nigeria, 2015 was the first year an opposition party gained power through elections. Botswana, Ghana, Cape Verde and Benin have also been lauded as democratic examples.

This year, at least 16 African nations are holding presidential elections. Although elections do not automatically lead to representative governments, competitive, multi-party elections constitute a sine qua non for democracy, and regular ballots indicate progress towards ensuring citizens are able to choose their leaders.

2. Africa Is Dominated by Big Men

A club of authoritarian leaders have maintained an iron grip on power in parts of Africa, either by amending laws to extend their terms of office, hosting rubber-stamp elections or repressing opposition and civil society. Of course, African countries are not alone in this—Singapore's founding father, Lee Kuan Yew, led for more than three decades; Cambodia's Hun Sen has also been in power for more than three decades; and in Kazakhstan, Nursultan Nazarbayev has held office since before the collapse of the Soviet Union.

In Africa, nine leaders have wielded power for more than 20 years; three of them have been at the helm for more than 30 years. Equatorial Guinea's President Teodoro Obiang Nguema Mbasogo seized power from his uncle in 1979, the same year that Angola's José Eduardo dos Santos rose to power. Yoweri Museveni won this month's election in Uganda to continue his rule after a vote marred by a lack of transparency.

But Africa is about more than this club of big men. Aside from the growing number of leaders passing power peacefully after elections, there have also been cases of public backlash against leaders who have tried to prolong their tenures, such as Zambia's Frederick Chiluba and Malawi's Bakili Muluzi. In 2014, Blaise Compaoré's bid to extend his 27-year presidency in Burkina Faso was thwarted by a violent popular uprising, while upheaval in Burundi was sparked by President Pierre Nkurunziza's successful bid to prolong his term.

Nor is leadership the sole preserve of men. In 2006, Liberia's Ellen Johnson Sirleaf became Africa's first democratically elected female head of state. She was followed by Joyce Banda in Malawi and Ameenah Gurib-Fakim in Mauritius.

Curiously, the Big Man moniker is generally applied only to African leaders. Some trace its roots to colonial masters and the choices they made when selecting rulers to succeed them after independence. As he prepared to step down as president in 2005, Tanzania's Benjamin Mkapa called for a new, home-grown democracy. "That Africa ended up with big men at State House is not entirely unrelated to this colonial legacy. Colonialists did not prepare Africans for self-democratic rule," Mkapa said.

3. Elections Are the Sole Indicator of a Thriving Democracy

Often the first things people point to as proof of democracy, elections are a precursor rather than the sole signifier of democratic rule.

When asked whether elections were giving democracy a bad name, former UN secretary general Kofi Annan said: "Democracy is not just about one day every four or five years when elections are held, but a system of government that respects the separation of powers, fundamental freedoms like the freedom of thought, religion, expression, association and assembly and the rule of law … Any regime that rides roughshod on these principles loses its democratic legitimacy, regardless of whether it initially won an election."

The Ibrahim index of African governance, an annual assessment produced by the Mo Ibrahim Foundation, focuses on what happens between elections. It defines good governance as safety and rule of law, participation by citizens and a respect for human rights, sustainable economic opportunity, and human development.

Topping the 2015 index were Mauritius, Cape Verde and Botswana. Central African Republic, South Sudan and Somalia—all nations torn by conflict—were bottom.

4. High Voter Turnout Means Corruption

A common perception is that high turnouts indicate fraud or ballot box stuffing. The reality is complex.

A reported 89% of Rwanda's voting population cast ballots in the most recent election in 2013. The party of President Paul Kagame, who has held his position for 16 years, won 93% of the vote. Was this a sign of a country freely giving a vote of approval to a popular leader, or a sign of coercion?

It is worth bearing in mind that 25 sub-Saharan African countries recorded voter turnouts of more than 50% at their last election, including in those widely viewed as democratic such as in Sierra Leone (88%), and Ghana (82%).

It's easy to judge turnout by western standards of voter apathy—turnout in the UK's general election in 2015 was 66%; in the US, turnout is usually even lower, at 54% in 2012. Yet younger democracies often have higher levels of political engagement, with citizens queueing for hours to make sure their votes count.

5. The Passing of Power Is Often Violent

When voters believe there has been election fraud, the risk of violence is high. In some cases the violence is initiated by incumbent leaders who feel threatened by opponents and incite protests, further destabilising their countries. Recent cases of electoral violence include Kenya's 2007 election which left 1,133 people dead, 600,000 people displaced and involved a wave of sexual violence, as well in Sierra Leone in 2007 and Senegal in 2012.

Violence can also be triggered when the opposition feel cheated at the ballot box, either because of fraud, coercion and intimidation. When citizens feel the judiciary will back the incumbent elite, they may be more inclined to take their protests to the streets. Other options exist elsewhere—the 2000 US election ended up in the courts after allegations of a miscount.

While the elections in Africa that garner the most international attention are often those that turn violent, many more are peaceful. Voters in Central African Republic went to the polls in February hoping to end years of conflict, and the presidential run-off took place peacefully despite months of sectarian and ethnic violence, albeit with a lower turnout.

Periodical and Internet Sources Bibliography

The following articles have been selected to supplement the diverse views presented in this chapter.

Jordan Bruneau, "Why Republicans Should Support Immigration," *New York Times*, January 2, 2019. https://www.nytimes.com/2019/01/02/opinion/trump-republicans-immigration.html.

Jenny Clark, "Seven Steps to Become a Global Citizen," GVI, 2018. https://www.gviusa.com/blog/7-steps-to-become-a-global-citizen.

European Youth Forum, "The Future of Education and Global Citizenship," June 26, 2014. https://www.youthforum.org/future-education-and-global-citizenship.

Johanna Flashman, "Global Citizenship: Saving the Nations," Quantumrun, March 7, 2017. https://www.quantumrun.com/article/global-citizenship-saving-nations.

Christina Fuleihan, "The Future of Global Citizenship," *Sandspur*, February 9, 2017. http://www.thesandspur.org/future-global-citizenship.

Juuso Jarviniemi, "Flexible Forms of Citizenship Are the Future," *New Federalist*, January 9, 2016. https://www.thenewfederalist.eu/flexible-forms-of-citizenship-are-the-future.

Neha Shah, "Mandela's Vision of Ending Extreme Poverty by Taking 5.6 Million Actions," Global Citizen, December 3, 2018. https://www.globalcitizen.org/en/content/mandela-100-impact-report-2018.

For Further Discussion

Chapter 1

1. How do you define citizenship?
2. What, if any, duties or obligations are involved in citizenship?
3. Why or why do you not believe in birthright citizenship?

Chapter 2

1. On what global issues can the activism of ordinary citizens make the greatest impact?
2. What can be done to alleviate fear of immigrants in Europe and the United States?
3. Why is active citizenship more difficult to achieve in some countries than others?

Chapter 3

1. How does social media affect the ability of people to create positive change?
2. Where in the world has evidence shown that social media can make a difference?
3. Do young people get unfair criticism about their desire to become active citizens?

Chapter 4

1. Do you foresee the eventuality of a world government? Why or why not?
2. How does income inequality around the world affect the effectiveness of citizenship?
3. Do you predict more or less engagement in activism globally in the future? Provide reasons for your answer using information from the viewpoints in this resource.

Organizations to Contact

The editors have compiled the following list of organizations concerned with the issues debated in this book. The descriptions are derived from materials provided by the organizations. All have publications or information available for interested readers. The list was compiled on the date of publication of the present volume; the information provided here may change. Be aware that many organizations take several weeks or longer to respond to inquiries, so allow as much time as possible.

Amnesty International USA
5 Penn Plaza, 16th Floor
New York, NY 10001
(800) AMNESTY
website: www.amnestyusa.org

Amnesty International USA seeks to engage people in the United States to fight injustice throughout the world while doing the same to protect the rights of the American people as well. The organization boasts more than one million members in the United States, who are part of a larger global movement of more than seven million in 150 countries.

CARE USA
151 Ellis Street NE
Atlanta, GA 30303
(800) 422-7385
email: info@care.org
website: www.care.org

CARE USA works to end famine and other deadly scourges, defeat poverty, and achieve social justice. It partners with corporations, institutions, and other agencies to make a difference in hard-hit regions of the world.

Carter Center

453 Freedom Parkway
Atlanta, GA 30307
(880) 550-3560
email: info@cartercenter.org
website: www.cartercenter.org

The mission of this organization, named after former American president Jimmy Carter, who had been actively involved, is to further the cause of human rights, work to resolve global conflicts while strengthening freedom, and improve health. The center is active in working to alleviate severe problems relating to the human condition.

Global Citizen

594 Broadway, Suite 207
New York, NY 10012
email: media@globalcitizen.org
website: www.globalcitizen.org

Global Citizen is a movement of engaged citizens working together in attempting to end extreme poverty by 2030. On its platform, global citizens are educated about the root and systemic causes of extreme poverty. They act on those issues and earn rewards for their work.

Human Rights Watch

350 Fifth Avenue
New York, NY 10118-3299
(212) 290-4700
website: www.hrw.org

This nonprofit organization promotes human rights around the world with a staff of global experts, lawyers, journalists, and academics of diverse nationalities. It issues reports on human rights abuses and meets with governments as well as regional groups to improve the lives of those in the international community.

OXFAM International

226 Causeway Street, 5th Floor
Boston, MA 02114
(800) 776-9326
website: www.oxfamamerica.org
email: info@oxfamamerica.org

OXFAM's mission is to fight poverty and social injustice. The organization works to help people empower themselves while fighting the roots of poverty and creating lasting solutions.

United Nations Educational, Scientific and Cultural Organization (UNESCO)

7, place de Fontenoy
75352 Paris 07 SP France
+33 0(1) 45 68 10 00
website: www.unesco.org

UNESCO works to create conditions for positive communication between cultures and peoples based on commonly shared values. It believes that only through such dialogue can the world achieve long-term peace while developing human rights, ending poverty, and gaining mutual respect.

United Nations Children's Fund (UNICEF)

125 Maiden Lane, 11th Floor
New York, NY 10038
(212) 686-5522
website: www.unicef.org
email: www.unicefusa.org/about/contact/email

UNICEF works in nearly two hundred countries and territories with a mission of helping less fortunate children of the world. The organization has helped save more children's lives than any other humanitarian group. It provides health care and immunizations, clean water and sanitary conditions, education, and emergency relief.

Bibliography of Books

Lee Watanabe Crockett and Andrew Churches, *Growing Global Digital Citizens: Better Practices That Build Better Learners*. Bloomington, IN: Solution Tree Press, 2017.

Garry Davis, *My Country Is the World: The Adventures of a World Citizen*. CreateSpace Independent Publishing Platform, 2010.

William Gaudelli, *Global Citizenship Education*. New York, NY: Routledge, 2016.

Mark Gerzon, *Global Citizens: How Our Vision of the World Is Outdated, and What We Can Do About It*. London, UK: Rider Books, 2010.

James E. Harf and Mark Owen Lombardi, *Taking Sides: Clashing Views on Global Issues*. Blacklick, OH: McGraw-Hill Education, 2016.

Silvia Hidalgo, *How to Be an American: A Field Guide to Citizenship*. New York, NY: Harry Abrams, 2018.

Martha S. Jones, *Birthright Citizens: A History of Race and Rights in Antebellum America*. Cambridge, UK: Cambridge University Press, 2018.

Christian Jopkke, *Citizenship and Immigration*. Boston, MA: Polity, 2010.

Kristen Mattson, *Digital Citizenship in Action: Empowering Students to Engage in Online Communities*. Arlington, VA: International Society for Technology in Education, 2017.

Claudia Rankine, *Citizen: An American Lyric*. Minneapolis, MN: Graywolf Press, 2014.

Fernando M. Reimers, Vidur Chopra, and Connie K. Chung, *Empowering Global Citizens*. CreateSpace Independent Publishing Platform, 2016.

Hans Schattle, *The Practices of Global Citizenship*. New York, NY: Rowman & Littlefield. 2007.

Solomon M. Skolnick, *The Great American Citizenship Quiz: Newly Revised and Updated*. New York, NY: Bloomsbury USA, 2017.

Index

O

P

R

S

T

U

V

W

Y